For Jane Austen
With
Admiration, Gratitude and my
Duty

Author's Note

When I began to write a mystery story set in the early 1800s in the form of a series of letters, I thought a splendid way to give it authenticity might be to interweave those of my heroine with the letters written by Jane Austen. Fully aware that this was a truly presumptuous thing to do, nevertheless I have plundered that treasure house—a most enjoyable occupation.

I hope the result will give those of my readers who already know the Austen letters the pleasure of recognition and, those who do not, the delight of discovery.

Someone once said that writing pastiche was like being lent an expensive and powerful motor car, which is thrilling to drive, but you're terrified of breaking it. I do hope I have returned this particular, wonderful vehicle in relatively pristine condition.

I have used the Brabourne Edition of the Letters, published in 1884 and dedicated to Queen Victoria, who was a great Jane Austen fan.

Hazel Holt, 1st July, 2009

Introduction

Hazel Holt has many devoted fans in the United States and Great Britain as a writer of "cosy" British mysteries; she has published nineteen Mrs. Malory novels at last count. She is also known to admirers of Barbara Pym as the friend and biographer who additionally edited Pym's posthumous works. This background of talent and expertise along with a deep appreciation of Jane Austen's novels and letters allows Holt to do what no one to my knowledge has attempted. She writes, as the title page announces, "with the assistance of Jane Austen's letters." That is, Holt brings together the style of the letters with a cast of characters that would be at home in Austen's novels, creating a work that offers pleasures that are the next best to those that an Austen novel affords.

Of course, you don't have to love Austen to love this book. If you enjoy detective novels, you will find here a completely satisfying murder mystery, coupled with a romance (or more than one, in fact). *My Dear Charlotte* gives you, in addition to mystery and romance, a portrait of the world of the English gentry at around 1815, immediately after the defeat of Napoleon—its manners and its moral certainty. As in Austen, Napoleon is not directly mentioned, but his shadow is there: one brother of the heroine is a sailor and the other a junior diplomat at the Congress of Vienna. It's the social world at home that is central, however, with its balls, visits, courtships, gossip, and of course murder, underlining the tensions and rifts within that apparently civilized society.

But it's readers of Jane Austen who will get the most pleasure from *My Dear Charlotte*. It is in my opinion the only successful attempt to re-create the **world** of Austen's novels, better even than the best of Georgette Heyer's Regency romances. Holt does much more, though: she has chosen to write a novel-in-letters, which allows her to incorporate witty quotations directly from Austen's letters into her novel, quotations about persons, occasions, the minutiae of daily life from housekeeping and shopping to the weather and human nature. Austen's comments take new meaning when they are thus placed in the context of this novel, in ways that I will hope to illustrate more fully later. Even without an added context, they can seem richer here, as in the following (taken from the 19th-century Brabourne edition of the letters):

> The masons are now repairing the chimney, which they found to be in such a state as to make it wonderful that it should have stood so long, and next to impossible that another violent wind should not blow it down. (MDC 29 Oct; JA Letters 7 Oct. 1808)

Seeing this line as a paragraph to itself, I finally appreciated its perfect evocation of the doom-laden pronouncements of repairmen, shaking their heads over the dismal condition of our fabric ("wonderful it should have stood so long") and over the heroic exertions they must undertake to save us before something like "another violent wind" occurs to our destruction. That is, Holt first of all makes the complicated ironies of Austen's letters more available to readers by taking them out of their original context and allowing us to focus on them.

What is even more important, however, is that the inclusion of such comments from Austen's letters dictates style. Unless you know those letters really well, you will simply not detect all of the quotations in *My Dear Charlotte*. The insertions are seamless because, astonishingly, Holt captures their tone and wit and language, their style, in fifty-five letters from her heroine Elinor Cowper (pronounced Cooper) to her sister, "My Dear Charlotte," over about seven months. And, as in Austen, style is character. Elinor has the qualities of Austen in the letters, an inquisitive, sharp, ironical eye that she turns on everything in her world—dress, food, family life, and in Elinor's case, murder. But because she is a character in a story, enmeshed in plot, she is more knowable than Jane Austen and more familiar. We inevitably read her through our understanding of Austen's characters, and as the novel progresses, Elinor the letter writer (or narrator) sounds more and more like Elizabeth Bennet, with the occasional dash of Mary Crawford's superior bitchiness. Her irony doesn't, then, have the "godlike impersonality" that some scholars attribute to Austen's narrators.[1] Instead, all Elinor writes reveals character, her own or others', even when she is producing sentences from Austen's letters. As an example, the line about the masons repairing the chimney shows Elinor's relish for the human foibles that lubricate society, keep it going—in this case, both the masons' enjoyment of the power their expertise gives them, stretching to exaggeration of danger, and also our own helpless and probably ignorant reliance on that expertise.

Often, the quotations from Austen's letters are placed firmly in the context of the mystery plot and do service there. After rejecting the idea that "chicken and asparagus fricassee" could have caused a suspicious death in another household, Elinor wonders what should be served to the magistrate at dinner:

> ...perhaps we should settle on having a plain roasted bird when Sir Edward comes to dine since any possible threat to a magistrate might put us in danger of the law.
>
> Our mother said that Mr Russell looked remarkably well—legacies are a very wholesome diet (MDC 26 July).

Austen's witty "legacies are a very wholesome diet"—pointing out how we selfishly thrive on what allegedly should grieve us—becomes even wittier in the context of genuine but also slightly absurd concern over what to feed the magistrate. The majesty of the law is thus mocked by appearing to preside over the wholesomeness of a dinner instead of inquiring into a possibly ill-gotten legacy. The reference to a chicken and asparagus fricassee will also make readers of *Emma* recall the "delicate fricassee of sweetbread and some

---

[1] Deirdre Lynch, "Jane Austen and Genius," A Companion to Jane Austen, ed. Claudia L. Johnson and Clara Tuite (Chichester, UK: Wiley-Blackwell, 2009), p.394.

asparagus,"[2] a favorite dish snatched away from poor Mrs. Bates by Mr. Woodhouse's concern for his own health. This subtle allusion to Austen's novel ties together the selfishness that can underlie hospitality with the selfishness of inheritance—not a "wholesome diet" at all.

As is evident, the pleasures of *My Dear Charlotte,* are increased the more one knows not just Austen's letters but her biography and the novels as well, particularly *Emma.* Those who know the biography will enjoy finding parallels and contrasts between Elinor and Austen herself, and between their sisters Charlotte and Cassandra. One of my favorite instances occurs when Elinor is describing to Charlotte the contents of a cupboard she had to empty. Among other childhood treasures, Elinor finds "the book of pressed ferns that occupied so much of your time until you wearied of it and turned your attention to collecting riddles" (MDC 16 Aug.). That Charlotte, who is more sedate and proper than Elinor and also a bit of a hypochondriac, should have collected riddles like *Emma's* Harriet Smith is perfect—and that Elinor should enjoy this slight jab at her beloved sister's pastimes reveals their real intimacy. While we know nothing of Cassandra Austen's pastimes other than her drawing, this line encourages me to reread Austen's letters for signs that she too has a sister who complains perhaps overmuch.

Though allusions to *Emma* are the most evident, it is of course not the only Austen novel that events and comments and characters and sometimes even passages in *My Dear Charlotte,* evoke. *Persuasion* is important also. The town closest to Elinor's home is Lyme, after all. Elinor's slightly hypochondriacal sister Charlotte is outdone by their married sister Mary who, as Elinor reports, "has had one of her bad throats this last month or more and, as we are aware, her throats are always worse than anyone's" (MDC 25 June): the whining Mary Musgrove of *Persuasion* is with us here almost word for word (see the postscript to Mary Musgrove's letter,

---

[2]   Here and elsewhere in this introduction, page numbers refer to R.W. Chapman's editions of Austen's novels.

p.164), and whining is a constant thread in *My Dear Charlotte* as a whole. But Holt manages to allude to *Persuasion* through just one word in the following passage—which doesn't at all quote Austen's letters—while also skewering various characters as well as the society that shapes them:

> Poor Miss Craven and her mama must have been sadly disappointed. Without Mrs Woodstock's eye upon him, Mr Russell exchanged the merest civilities with them and made his escape as soon as he decently could. But Miss Craven may still find a husband. She is, for the most part, silent and not ill-looking if one can overlook her freckles, and I am sure that may easily be done by contemplation of her fortune, so I shall not feel sorry for her. (MDC 26 Aug.)

It's the word "freckles" that brings in Mrs. Clay of *Persuasion* and Sir Walter Elliot's delusions about them—first that her freckles are impossible to overlook, rendering Mrs. Clay hopelessly unattractive, and second that they have been erased by his recommendation of Gowland's lotion. Mrs. Clay has no fortune to make her freckles vanish—whereas, in the society of *Persuasion* and *My Dear Charlotte,* fortune makes any woman able to find a husband, especially a woman who, tellingly, is "silent" and "not ill-looking." In this world, such a woman's fortune nicely alliterates with and cancels out her freckles. Though we never learn the precise amount of Elinor's fortune (or that of Charlotte), nor indeed what she looks like (though she is evidently attractive), we discover that her father's estate of Monkton near Lyme is worth £2000 a year (MDC 5 Nov.)—an essential detail in the world of *My Dear Charlotte,* as in any of the Austen novels.

One final instance of the rich and complex relation between this novel and Austen's: Elinor thus reports her mother's rhapsodies on Mr. Rivers—

> 'Why, when Mrs Brompton was laid up with a cold he went all the way to Exeter to procure some special wool she needed to complete a carpet she was making. And when he dined with us he was able to converse easily with Mr Mildmay, who is quite deaf and needs a good deal of trouble to make him hear—a great problem on

such occasions, and I have often said to Mr Cowper that only the fact that he is one of our oldest friends persuades me to invite him! No, Mr Rivers is a splendid addition to our society and I for one will be very sorry to see him go back to Barbados.' (MDC 19 Sept.)

Character is finely rendered here. Mrs. Cowper is a little like Miss Bates in her loquacity and sometimes even like Mrs. Bennet her bare-faced manipulativeness. In this instance, the good-hearted, open tone of Miss Bates's voice seems to prevail, but it is possible that when we arrive at "a great problem" and "I have often said to Mr Cowper" we can hear in our minds something of the fretfulness of Mrs. Bennet. That is, when dialogue is reported, as here, the tone remains ambiguous, like the tone of Darcy's remarks to Elizabeth in the first volume of *Pride and Prejudice:* on first reading, we are likely to hear that tone as haughty, as Elizabeth does; on subsequent readings, we may hear the same words as more friendly, more interested, more attracted. Holt's dialogue in this novel has some of that same Austenian ambiguity, inviting rereading.

Comedy is also finely rendered in this passage. What is delightful here is the way that Mrs. Cowper reveals that she herself is the gold standard of politeness: only because Mr. Mildmay is such an old friend will **she** invite him, so that Mr. Rivers' civility elevates him to her own moral high ground. In this passage, the moral certainty of Mrs. Cowper is treated comically, but the social world described is one in which such judgments are constantly made, with a freedom that seems alien in our own world. Not that such judgments are necessarily correct. Here, as in Austen's novels, sometimes even the most confident judges, proud of their discernment, like Elizabeth Bennet or indeed like Elinor Cowper, make mistakes.

In these passages and just about any others chosen at random from *My Dear Charlotte,* readers can appreciate how far Holt's choice to base her novel on Austen's letters dictates its tone, wit, and language, and how far her choice to mine Austen's novels to provide paradigms for characters, courtships, and moral qualities, dictates its overall comedy. To all this, Holt adds a murder mystery, used (as is traditional) to underline the inequity that the social world is partly based upon, however many admirable individuals populate it. Holt depicts this class-based historical community without nostalgia. Though the main characters are of the gentry, all the classes are there and shown to be interdependent. The relations among the classes, how they each affect one another, are carefully sketched, but the murder and some of the unpleasant characters indicate a fundamental corruption that precludes a nostalgic presentation of community, of the world we have lost.

Because readers will enjoy finding their own parallels to the novels and to Austen's own family, as well as their own favorite comic moments, I have been sparing in my examples. I have also tried to avoid spoiling the various plots by giving too many details. With great confidence, I recommend to you the pleasures of reading and rereading *My Dear Charlotte*.

Jan Fergus
Professor of English Emerita, Lehigh University

Principal Characters

Residing at Lyme Regis:

 Henry Cowper, gentleman (pronounced "Cooper")

 Mrs. Cowper, his wife

 Charlotte Cowper, their elder daughter, away on visits

 Elinor Cowper, their younger daughter, letter writer

 Frank Cowper, their son, in Vienna with the diplomatic corps

 William Cowper, their son, on duty with the Royal Navy

 Lucy maidservant to the Cowpers and sister to Sarah, housekeeper at Holcombe Park

 Mrs. and Miss Caroline West, new residents at Chilton House by the Cobb, Lyme

 Maria Brompton and Mrs. Holder, who know all that goes on in and around Lyme

 Rugeley's book shop and Layton's haberdashery, where Lyme residents often call

At Holcombe Park:

 Mr. Woodstock, gentleman

 Mrs. Woodstock, invalid

 Sir Matthew Russell, Mrs. Woodstock's brother, an eminent physician

 Mr. James Russell, Mrs. Woodstock's nephew, and nephew to Sir Matthew Russell, on a visit from London

 Mr. Frederick Rivers, Mr. Woodstock's cousin and estate manager in Barbados, on a visit

 Corbett, Mr. James Russell's valet

 Chapman, Mrs. Woodstock's maid

 Sarah, Mrs. Woodstock's housekeeper

At Marshwood Abbey:

 Sir Edward Hampton of Hatch Beauchamp and Marshwood Abbey, justice of the peace

 George and John Hampton, his young sons

 Miss Blair, their governess

 Mrs. Hodges, housekeeper to Sir Edward

My Dear Charlotte

My Dear Charlotte,

Your letter this morning was quite unexpected and disappointed me of my first sentence which I had planned, full of proper hopes about your journey. I was sorry to hear that your trunk was too heavy to go by the coach from Taunton, but you were fortunate to find a wagon that could convey it all the way to Bath. I do indeed hope that you may not have taken cold after your stop at Shepton Mallet, but I have often found the brief introduction of a warming pan into cold sheets does provoke the *feeling* of dampness without the actual ill effects.

I am glad that our uncle has settled on a house in Green Park Buildings since the one that he and our aunt took last year in New King Street had pitifully small rooms. You may remember that the best of the sitting rooms was not as large as our parlour here. Those at G.P. Buildings are quite spacious and *dry* since I believe that no inconvenience from the river may be felt there. So I shall think of you happily established with a fire in your room and every kind of comfort about you.

I was surprised at your news that bonnets of cambric muslin are much worn in Bath and that there are a multitude of black gauze cloaks. Our mother has ordered a new bonnet; white stripe with white ribbon, while I shall continue with my old straw bonnet which I fancy is as smart as other people's.

My news is of a less elevated order, namely that Mrs Woodstock has taken to her old tricks of ill health again and, pronouncing herself to be dying once more, has ordered her nephew James Russell post haste from London to attend upon her. So our circle will be enlarged by one, and since he seems an agreeable young man (you will recall his being so obliging, the last time he was at one of our assemblies, to stand up with me for two of the dances) I for one am delighted at her indisposition.

We dine now at half after three, and have done dinner I suppose before you begin. We drink tea at half past six—I am afraid that when you return you will despise us.

Some of the flower seeds are coming up very well, but the pinks and mignonette make a wretched appearance. By the blossom we are likely to have a great crop of Orleans plums, but not many greengages. Your hens show no sign of missing you and continue to lay with great prodigality. Adieu—I must leave off to stir the fire and call on Miss Williams.

Yr affectionate sister,
Elinor Cowper

My Dear Charlotte,

This will be a quick return for yours: I doubt it having much else to recommend it. I am sorry that your poor ankle prevented you from walking in the Crescent fields with Miss Winstone, but if the wind was cold perhaps it was as well you forwent the pleasure. It was fortunate that you had your new paisley shawl as well as your pelisse when you went to the Rooms with our uncle. I do trust that our aunt will soon be free of her bilious fever and hope that you do not feel obliged to follow the fashion she has set.

I do have one brand new item of news for you. A Mrs West and her daughter have taken Chilton's house by the Cobb. It is said that Miss West has been ill and has been advised to seek the beneficial effects of sea air. They come, it seems, from Kent and I would have thought that there would be sea air enough in that county to suffice, but perhaps it has not such a benevolent quality as that at Lyme. I should not complain of any addition to our company, although I have heard that Miss West, illness notwithstanding, is reckoned to be exceptionally good looking, so we may find ourselves eclipsed by the presence of a distinguished Beauty in our midst.

Henry Wilmot called yesterday to visit our father and stayed to drink tea with us. He is sadly accommodated at Charton, such a poor parish, a miserable house and less than £50 a year. If only he could get the curacy of Westover he would be made, but although the living is in Mr Woodstock's gift, the whole world knows that it is *Mrs* Woodstock's dislike of Mr Wilmot's Evangelicalism that holds him back from this felicity. Though our father, as you know, is fond of Mr Wilmot (in spite of his forever quoting the more extreme opinions of Mr Wesley) still I thought that yesterday even he was somewhat taken aback by our guest's *enthusiasm*. But I feel Mr Wilmot is a good man, forever on the lookout for some means of alleviating the wretchedness of the many needy souls in his charge and I wish he had a wife who might help to alleviate some of his, for he lives very poorly, and apart from the satisfaction of converting an obdurate parishioner, appears to have very little that might pass for happiness in his life.

If you will send our father an account of your washing and letter expenses etc, he says he will send you a draft for the amount of it as well as money for your next quarter. If you do not buy that gown of china crape now, on the strength of this, I shall never forgive you.

We have finished 'The Female Quixote' and our father is now reading Crabbe's "The Borough" once more for our evening's entertainment. Rugeley the bookseller has promised that Miss Edgeworth's latest work which he has at his Bridport shop will be at Lyme next week and also Mr Bickerstaff's play "The Hypocrite," if Mrs Jennings at Uplyme shall have returned it.

I hope your weather has been more agreeable than the variety we are enjoying here (though we both know that an umbrella is, of course, a prime necessity in Bath). The rain has been woefully persistent and I am feeling 'cabin'd, cribb'd, confined' by being limited to walking in the shrubbery these last few days. However the Lythams did brave the shocking roads to drink tea and play cribbage so we have not been left quite to our own resources. They have heard from their son John who is at Gibraltar and was thus able to give us news of the *Scorpion*. He had seen William and mentioned him in his letter in such terms as to relieve all our minds of anxiety and give great comfort and satisfaction to our mother.

It seems likely that William may be there for a little while yet, so that it might be possible to send his shirts as they are finished; one set could go this week. Mr Lytham who, as you know, has the ear of Admiral Gambier was most hopeful of William's prospects.

I hear from Martha who desires her best love and says a great many kind things about spending some time with you when you go to Robert and Mary later.

Your affectionate sister,
E.C.

My Dear Charlotte,

I was astonished to hear how inhumanly thin of company the Upper rooms were—though the people there would have made five or six very pretty Lyme assemblies. I am glad that it *cheered up* after tea and that you were able to link the Winstones onto your party. I am sure that your muslin was greatly enhanced by the plaited white satin ribbon with the pearl edge, which must have made it practically a new gown. Was Mrs Winstone expensively and nakedly dressed, as she was when I saw her last? I was glad to hear that Mrs Maitland's disorder had not ended fatally as you had feared and that she was pronounced out of danger last Sunday.

Did you think of our ball last Tuesday and did you suppose me at it? On Monday morning it was settled that I should go with Mrs Holder and in the afternoon she sent to ask if I should mind if Mrs West and her daughter Caroline were of the party. You may imagine that I was delighted to have the opportunity of observing the Beauty at close quarters and you will also have guessed that I spent extra care on my choice of gown (the muslin with the glossy spot) and desired Lucy to curl my hair high up so that I might wear a band of the same muslin about my head.

I was by no means disappointed in Miss West's appearance. She is tall and decidedly handsome with golden hair (dressed á la Grèque) and large blue eyes. I would guess that she is nineteen or twenty and, as far as I could see, bore no trace of illness of any kind. Indeed her step was positively *sprightly*—she was wearing the most elegant white slippers—and she stood up for nine of the dances, of which there were only twelve. I danced ten and was merely prevented from dancing the rest by the want of a partner.

Miss West was all that was amiable and determined to be friendly.

"Do you read much, Miss Cowper?" she asked. "I am very fond of reading."

I agreed that reading was a pleasant pastime.

"Have you read "Udolpho," Miss Cowper? Is it not an excellent book?"

I confirmed her opinion.

"And do you care for walking, Miss Cowper?" she enquired. Mrs Holder being present declared that I was a great one for walking, even in the dirtiest of weather.

"Then," said Miss West "perhaps we could walk together, since I am sure there are many delightful walks in the neighbourhood, if you will be kind enough to shew them to me."

Mrs Holder seized upon this idea with all the enthusiasm of one who is not to be involved and so I am committed to an hour's insipid conversation tomorrow. Perhaps I may be permitted to learn what the mysterious illness was and why the air of Kent was not considered sufficient to ensure a full recovery from it, though this intelligence will hardly compensate me for such tedium.

The Misses Cox paid us a morning visit and from them we learned that James Russell is expected on Saturday, so I will hope to have more interesting news to give you in my next letter to balance the report of my excursion with Miss West.

I hear that Mr Littlemore is to be married to a very agreeable young lady, rich in music and money. I met her at the Chamberlynes once and found her like any other tall girl with a wide mouth, large nose and fashionable dress. However, Mr Littlemore can count himself fortunate to get her since, although he is a gentlemanlike young man, his legs are too short.

We all unite in love and I am affectionately yours,
E.C.

My Dear Charlotte,

My expectations of Miss West were not disappointed. We were on the Cobb for an hour together, she having rejected my suggestion of a walk towards Charmouth.

"I adore walking, Miss Cowper," she said "indeed I am never happier than when so engaged, but the roads here are so very bad, quite unlike our roads in Kent which are clear even in the worst of winter." And so it was—a paean of praise for every aspect of Kentish life and everything at Lyme quite disparaged, which makes me wonder all the more what brings her to this despised place.

She is amazingly affable.

"I declare that is a delightful spencer you are wearing, Miss Cowper, kerseymere is so comfortable on such a brisk spring day as this. The sea air is so strong that I had barely stepped from our front door when I was obliged to return for my fur tippet. And such a charming purse; did you net it yourself? Is there a good draper here in Lyme? I am sadly short of knotting silk and gold paper. Do you know, I was so distressed to find that my silver embroidery scissors have been lost in our removal here. They were a present from a very dear friend and I value them greatly. I do not suppose that such a pair are to be had in Lyme." And so on, until Miss West declared that the wind coming off the sea was too strong for her to stand upright (it was the merest breeze) and we walked back to her house.

Like some young ladies Miss West is genteeler than her parent (I mean Mrs West since I have not yet discovered if there be a Mr West) who sat darning a pair of stockings the whole of my visit. She is a large-faced woman, of ample figure and dressed in grey but with black ribbons on her gown and cap, so perhaps Mr West is no more. She has an effusive manner of speech and rattles away with scarcely a pause for breath between the sentences and certainly no gap into which anyone else could conveniently drop a word. I sat as long as civility required and then thankfully made my escape without committing myself to another expedition, using your absence as an excuse for my busyness at home.

Indeed, it is no more than the truth since our mother is at present suffering from a cold which affects her in the usual way. Dr King called yesterday to see her and I hope she will soon physic away the worst part of it. Meanwhile I have taken on the housekeeping and am much tormented by thoughts of haunches of mutton and apple dumplings. I ordered three pair of small soles and although they only had a short journey to make from the harbour they cost the best part of three shillings. I have carefully concealed from our mother the intelligence you sent me that meat in Bath is only 8d a pound and cheese 9d, but I may let her know that salmon is 2s.9d. per pound the whole fish.

Lucy, thank goodness, is an excellent servant and greatly eases my burden, not least by her ready flow of information which keeps me amused during some of our more tedious household tasks. She tells me that Mrs Woodstock has turned away their coachman John, for no other reason than a slight delay in bringing round the carriage last month which, Lucy avows, was by no means his fault. This is particularly unfortunate since he was to marry Lucy's sister Sarah, who, you will recall, is the Woodstock's housekeeper, and now there will be no marriage since there is not money enough and, after such a dismissal, he will find it difficult to get another position in this neighbourhood. Lucy, by the by, does not think the mead in a state yet to be stopped down.

I forgot to say that I was in such a state of frustration after my miserable amble with Miss West that the next morning I walked the greater part of the way to Uplyme to visit Fanny Grafton, who among other more trivial items of news, told me that Mr Edmund Moore is to have the living of Kilmington and will thus be practically our neighbour. Now do not tell me that this news does not cause your heart to flutter a little. At least it will greatly increase our interest in the Axminster assemblies.

Mr James Russell is looked for tomorrow. We must hope that his delay in attending upon his aunt will not cause him to be turned away like poor John. I will keep you informed upon this and other important matters in my next letter. But now Lucy has come in asking for more soap so I must leave off and seek the storeroom key which I laid down I know not where this morning. So you see how greatly you are missed and what a poor creature is in your place.

My mother desires her love to you all.

Yours affectionately,
E.C.

My Dear Charlotte,

My expectation of having more news for you being fulfilled, I lay aside my household duties to keep you properly informed.

Mr James Russell did indeed arrive yesterday, having been delayed, so my intelligence has it, by a broken trace the other side of Devizes. This apparently being considered a sufficient excuse, he is allowed to stay and be a comfort to his aunt's declining days, though I do not think her yet to be upon her death bed since we have this morning received an invitation—nay a Command—to dine at Holcombe Park.

Later this morning, as I was coming out of Layton's (very pretty English poplins at 4s 3d; Irish ditto at 6s, more pretty, quite beautiful), I was able to see for myself that Mr Russell is indeed in Lyme, for there he was standing looking into the window of Rugeley's shop, apparently perusing fine volumes of "Sir Charles Grandison" most elegantly bound with a great deal of gold leaf. He turned as I approached and, to my surprise, greeted me with the warmth of an old friend.

"Miss Cowper! Just the person I had wished to see. I hope you will spare the time to take a walk with me so that I may learn all that has happened in this delightful place since I was here last year."

I was decidedly taken aback since we had not been on such terms on his previous visit to warrant such a greeting. Nevertheless my curiosity (which you know to be greater than average) impelled me to walk with him along the promenade for half an hour. I will not conceal from you, dear Charlotte, the impulse of pleasure one feels from walking beside the sea on a fine spring morning with an agreeable young man. Mr Russell is of no great height (indeed I remember your remarking upon it when he was here) but being of slight build and with rather delicate features he has a most gentlemanlike appearance, especially since he was wearing what I take to be the most elegant London fashion. You may imagine that I was glad to be wearing my olive green pelisse and a new bonnet with the pleated lining so that I felt fit to be seen with him.

"I do hope," I said, "that your aunt is improved in health."

"Why yes," he replied with a laugh. "You must know that once whatever fancy she has indulged in has been fulfilled, she makes a rapid recovery."

You will feel, as I did, that although this might be true (as we all know that it is) still, it was not a proper way for him to be talking of his aunt.

"We will look forward to seeing her" I said, "when we dine at Holcombe Park tomorrow."

"It will be our pleasure" he said warmly, "to welcome you and your family. I have persuaded my aunt that there should be dancing after dinner and I do hope that you and your sister will have the kindness to stand up with me."

I explained that you were staying with our aunt and uncle in Bath.

"And you, Miss Cowper, do you not feel envious of your sister enjoying the pleasures of Bath?"

"It is a most agreeable town" I replied "and I greatly enjoyed the time we spent there last year, but I like to be away from so much bustle and nearer to the countryside in the spring."

"You care for the beauties of Nature, then" he said. "I daresay you are able to quote me whole passages of "The Seasons" by heart!"

I did not comment and he went on, "But tell me about Lyme. Are all my friends from last year still here?"

"Several have been removed by Death," I said. "Mr Staines of Uphill died last winter and Mrs Dawlish but a few weeks ago. The Eggertons have removed to Exeter and the Tenbys to Wells, so you see what a great deal of movement there is in Lyme society."

"And are there any new faces?" he asked.

"Indeed," I said, "our numbers have recently been increased by a Mrs West and her daughter who have taken a house by the Cobb. Miss West," I added, "has been ill and has been recommended the sea air by her physician."

"Miss West, then, is a lady of middle years and her mother quite elderly. Not companions for you and your sister?"

"On the contrary, I believe Miss West to be no more than twenty and a considerable beauty."

"Indeed," he said, "I shall eagerly await my first glimpse of this prodigy."

"Then, sir!" I replied "your patience will not be very severely tested since she is even now approaching."

Miss West was walking with Maria Brompton, who, as you know, is always eager to take up any newcomer so that she may be the first to know all their business and thus be in a position to enlighten others.

Maria exclaimed at seeing Mr Russell. Indeed he was not looked for until next week, or so she had heard, and how had he found his aunt, all Lyme had been concerned to hear that she was unwell and how fortunate that he had arrived so quickly since the weather had been rough and the roads were in a shocking state, she wondered that something could not be done to improve matters, travelling by postchaise or mail-coach was vastly disagreeable but no doubt in one's own carriage...

Miss West was looking very fine in a cerulean blue round gown with half boots in a matching colour and the freshness of the air had given her complexion a singular bloom so that I felt that Mr Russell could not but be struck with her beauty. I managed to find a pause in Maria's chatter and introduced him to Miss West. But alas, if I expected some expression of admiration to manifest itself, as one might find in fiction when a personable young man is first introduced to a beauty, I was disappointed for they exchanged the merest civilities. Miss West, indeed, seemed quite preoccupied and, after these few words hurried Maria away saying that she had to collect some letters from the post office.

"So that is your beauty," Mr Russell said. "I admit that many people would describe her so, but for myself I find fair hair insipid and much prefer dark hair and a brown complexion."

I do not scruple to tell you, My Dear Charlotte, that one's heart warms to such a man.

I had a letter yesterday from Mary saying that she fully intended writing to you by Mr Stevens' frank and only happened entirely to forget it, but will write to you soon. I will write to you after tomorrow's visit to Holcombe Park so that you may be fully informed of every detail of that great event. To you, of course, surrounded by the pleasures of Bath (did you enjoy your airing in that very bewitching phaeton and four and did you go to the top of Kingsdowne or was that considered too far?), they will seem but small beer.

Our father was delighted with the stockings, which are an excellent fit and most handsome, and desires me to tell you so. Adieu.

Yr affectionate sister,
E.C.

My Dear Charlotte,

If you paid attention to the conclusion of my last letter, you will be, I hope, eager to learn how all went off at Holcombe Park yesterday. Fortunately our father was able to spare the horses from the farm so we went in the carriage and did not need to set out until just before four o'clock. Mrs Woodstock, you will remember, dines fashionably at five.

We were sixteen: Mr and Mrs Woodstock, she seemingly recovered though very red in the face (I hope she may not be dropsical), he as mute and retiring as ever in his wife's company, Mr James Russell, Sir Thomas Egerton and his lady, who was wearing a most odd cap with a peak at the front and a multitude of beaded ribbon bows, two at the temples and one over the right ear, old Lady Newton, much improved by a new wig, Admiral Lloyd, who is grown very stout, Dr Matlock, now sadly deaf (I have heard that he can barely conduct a service and mistakes the timing of all the responses), Captain Tilson, whose red coat was very cheering in such company, Mr and Mrs Craven and their daughter Elizabeth, whose red hair and freckles were not enhanced by a gown of pink satin with a heavy lace overdress—though since her fortune is as extensive as her freckles I do not suppose that she needs to care about such things. There was one unfamiliar face, a tall gentleman, no longer in his first youth, though by no means middle-aged, with regular features, a very brown complexion and a most pleasant manner. He is, it appears, a Mr Frederick Rivers, a cousin of our host, who has been for some years in charge of Mr Woodstock's estates in Barbados. A bad fever necessitated his return to this country, which return must have been very recent indeed to have escaped our local intelligence. It was generally felt that his presence gave an agreeable novelty to the whole proceedings. The party was completed by Mr and Mrs Cowper and their daughter Elinor (wearing the yellow gauze gown and the long sleeves that you yourself admit may now be worn at evening parties).

You were enquired for very prettily, and I hope the whole assembly now understands that you are in Bath. Admiral Lloyd surpassed the rest in his attentive recollection of you and desired to be remembered to you when I wrote next, which instruction I have hereby carried out. After dinner (the widgeon with ginger was excellent, but the mutton shockingly underdone) Miss Craven was called upon to delight us with her playing upon the pianoforte, which she did at considerable length. Mr Russell stood dutifully at her side, turning the pages of her music while she sang a number of excessively mournful Scottish ballads.

It is obvious that Mrs Woodstock has made it plain to her nephew where his inclination should lie and it was entertaining to see how assiduous were his attentions to Miss Craven while his aunt's eye was upon him.

The larger part of the company made up tables to play quadrille, leaving only three couple to dance—Lady Egerton choosing to place herself in the *younger* set. Mr Russell led out Miss Craven, Lady Egerton, with that eye for a red coat you have often remarked on, partnered Captain Tilson, and I stood up with Mr Rivers. I found him very gentlemanlike and conversable and he tells a story well. He had many interesting things to say about life in Barbados, yet told with a liveliness and humour and not in the least dull or prosy. I danced several times with Captain Tilson and twice with Mr Russell (when his aunt's eye was occupied with her cards). In fact I cannot remember an evening at Holcombe Park passing so pleasantly, indeed, I was surprised when the tray was brought in for supper, to find it already 10 o'clock.

Our father was greatly taken with Mr Rivers, having had some conversation with him at dinner, and pronounced him a most sensible man. He (Mr Rivers) is to stay at Holcombe for a while to recover his strength before he returns to Barbados. From the conversation I had with him, I believe he loves that country and, indeed, he made it sound amazingly attractive, something I would not have believed possible. Our father was so struck with Mr Rivers that he has invited him to dine with us when the Chamberlynes come next week.

Our mother confirms my opinion that Mrs Woodstock has decided that her nephew is to marry Miss Craven—the Cravens' estate marches with that of the Woodstocks—so I imagine that the poor young man's fate is sealed. Certainly he can look for no support from his uncle—that wretched man would not dare to say boo to a goose, let alone his formidable spouse. I suppose Mr Russell might make a hasty return to London, but since he is solely dependent upon his aunt's bounty, I do not think such an action very likely. I daresay they will manage as well as others in the same situation. I do not believe Miss Craven disagreeable, though I have never found her intelligence to be great and her conversation is amazingly dull.

I shall be interested to see if our two new arrivals—Miss West and Mr Rivers—are at the Assembly next Thursday. Certainly illness did not appear to interfere with Mr Rivers' dancing and perhaps Miss West may find the exercise beneficial. Perhaps the fact of their both having been invalids will draw them together. I shall also look forward to the Assembly as being the occasion of my wearing the new lace you have so generously sent, the beauty of which astonished me—it is almost too handsome to be worn. I had hoped to dazzle the company at Holcombe in it, but unfortunately Mrs Dean has not yet attached it to my lilac muslin, but she promises it faithfully for Wednesday and I shall see that she does not fail.

The glasses have arrived (none broken) and have given great satisfaction. Our mother sends her thanks and wonders if you would kindly investigate the possibility of purchasing a mangle such as Mary obtained last time she was in Bath and which has proved such a success.

You will be happy to know that we had the felicity of a letter from William. I am glad to say that the *Scorpion* is still at Gibraltar. He has not yet received the shirts and I have hopes that he may stay there at least until they arrive. Lord Egerton said yesterday that he had read in the newspaper that all 1st Lieutenants of the frigates whose Captains were to be sent into line-of-battle ships, were to be promoted to the rank of Commanders. If Mr Layton's intelligence should be correct and William be transferred to a frigate soon ... but as you are aware there are two unreliable sources here—Sir Thomas Egerton and the newspapers!

I most finish now as Henry Wilmot is expected this forenoon. I hear from Eliza that he gave an excellent sermon last Sunday—a little too eager sometimes in his delivery, but that is better than a want of animation, especially when it comes from the heart as it does with him.

Yours affectionately,
E.C.

My Dear Charlotte,

Your letter took me by surprise this morning; you are very welcome, however, and I am obliged to you. I am sorry to hear that our uncle is no better for drinking the waters nor from the bathing. Perhaps now that he has transferred to Dr Fellowes from Dr Mapleton there will be some improvement, especially since, as you say, Dr Fellowes has become quite the most fashionable physician in Bath, and *that* we know is a powerful incentive for recovery in a patient. It is fortunate that this set-back has not in any way curtailed your entertainment. The grand gala in Sydney Gardens must have been charming with the concert, illuminations and fireworks. I am glad you were not cheated of this, as when you said the whole thing had been put off because of bad weather last week I had not realised it was merely postponed.

I am quite pleased with Isabella and Mrs Dean for wanting the pattern of our caps, but I am not so well pleased with your giving it to them. Rugeley called today with the books he promised. We have the second series of Miss Edgeworth's "Fashionable Life" as well as the Bickerstaffe and he produced a surprise—three volumes of Mrs Grant's "Memoirs of an American Lady" which he had extracted from Colonel Forrester's wife when he took a parcel of books to the militia camp on his way from his Bridport shop last Tuesday. I shall have these delights to myself at present since our mother has got Sir John Carr's "Travels in Spain" from Miss Lytham and is reluctant to break off for any new volume.

I had a brief conversation with James Russell yesterday when I was sheltering from a squally shower in Layton's shop. I expressed surprise at seeing him in a linendraper's and he replied, "A commission for my aunt, Miss Cowper. Some embroidery thread for a firescreen that she has been working this twelve-month to my certain knowledge."

"I trust, sir, that your aunt is now quite recovered. She seemed in excellent health when we had the pleasure of dining with you."

"Since she has now had her own way for seven days in a row, she is in excellent health and spirits," he replied lightly.

"I must say," he continued, "how much I enjoyed that occasion." I was wondering if he had been so obliging to his aunt as to fall in love with Miss Craven when he added, "Your presence, Miss Cowper, elevated a humdrum dinner party into an event of unique pleasure."

So you see, My Dear Charlotte, that Mr Russell is a confirmed flirt. He very kindly escorted me home since he had had the forethought to provide himself with an umbrella, and, when he came in to pay his respects to our mother, she took a sly delight in quizzing him about Miss Craven, in a roundabout way, you understand, but enough to tease him.

"It was such a pleasure to see Miss Craven in looks" she said.

"Indeed Miss Craven looked delightfully" was the reply.

"And she sang quite charmingly."

"Miss Craven is a very accomplished young lady." And so on. It was highly entertaining. Our father then spoke of Mr Rivers.

"We had not heard of his arriving; it was a pleasure to meet him."

"Frederick had not been looked for until the autumn," Mr Russell said "but the fact of his illness brought his visit forward. He has been the manager of my uncle's estate for many years now and this is his first visit to Holcombe. He is a very agreeable fellow."

"We must hope that our good Dorset air will soon make him well," our mother said.

"It certainly seems to have had a good effect upon Miss West," I said. "She is in fine spirits and will, I hope, be well enough to attend the next Assembly on Wednesday. Do you go, sir?"

"If *you* are going, Miss Cowper," he replied with a bow, "then I will certainly make a point of doing so."

"Oh everyone will be there," our mother said. "We sometimes have as many as four and thirty couple."

"Then I must immediately bespeak two dances with Miss Cowper here, for I am sure she will be engaged for all of them." So I have the comfort of being certain of one partner on Wednesday.

I forgot to mention that Rugeley told us that the—Militia is to move to Worthing and their place will be taken by the—Foot. We will certainly miss Captain Davey and Captain Barton at our Assemblies, but perhaps the—Foot may have in its ranks equally charming dancing partners. Indeed, unless one should happen to be personally attached to the wearer, one red coat is very like another.

I hear from Mary that her new nursery maid is a disappointment and will not suit, so the whole business is to be done again. I do hope that by the time of your visit a satisfactory substitute may have been found, though, knowing Mary's determination not to like anything or anyone recommended by her mama-in-law, it seems that the infant will be breeched and indeed in school before such a paragon may be obtained.

I must away to Mrs Dean to see whether or no my newly trimmed gown may be ready for the Assembly.

Your affectionate sister,
E.C.

My Dear Charlotte,

I was so sorry that you were not here to enjoy what was the best Assembly of the season. There were more dancers than the room could conveniently hold, which as you know is a sure recipe for success, and a very general want of chairs in the supper room. There were twenty dances and I danced all of them—without any fatigue I hasten to add, before you can ask! Thanks to your beautiful lace, my gown was as much acclaimed as if it had been a new one. However, Miss West was generally acknowledged to be the handsomest person present, her pink gauze with silver thread was openly admired by Maria Brompton and secretly, I imagine, by every other lady present. Mr Rivers seemed much struck with her and claimed two dances, as did Captain Tilson. James Russell, under the watchful eye of his aunt (in diamonds and a prodigious purple turban) divided his attentions between Miss Craven, Miss Terry and myself. He is as accomplished at dancing as he is at flirting and makes a very agreeable partner on both accounts.

You will be wondering if James Russell did indeed dance with Miss West. The answer is yes, but I had the impression that he would rather not have done so, but was obliged to approach her by Mrs Holder, who seems to have taken the Wests under her wing. Seeing Mr Russell who had just emerged from the card room where he had been attending on his aunt she said, "Why Mr Russell, I declare you haven't met Miss West who has just come to Lyme."

"I have already had the pleasure of meeting Miss West" he said quite formally and not at all in his lively manner.

Miss West smiled and cast down her eyes and there was a moment's silence, after which he could hardly, in good manners, do other than to ask her to dance. I do not think they danced together after that. I stood up for one of the country dances and the boulangere with Mr Rivers and you will not be surprised to learn that I could not help questioning him.

"I wonder, sir, if there are many occasions for dancing in Barbados?"

"Indeed" he said "there are quite often evening parties, though sometimes there may not be enough couples to make up a set for dancing."

"There are some ladies there, however?"

"Indeed," he replied "most of the estate owners and their managers are married and have families on the island."

"But you are not married, sir?" I ventured.

"I am a widower" he said.

This surprised me greatly since he does not at all *look* like a widower. "I am sorry, sir," I said. "I hope it was not a recent loss?"

"It was two years ago." He sighed. "Poor Maria caught a fever—not unusual, alas, in that climate, as I myself can vouch for—and died within a few days."

"Did your wife come out from England?" I asked.

"No, she was born in Barbados; she was the only daughter of Mr Richard Bridges, who owns the next estate to the one I manage. When Maria died they took our son John to bring up as their own, since he will one day have what should have been her inheritance."

This sad tale occupied me much, as you can imagine. You might suppose him quite justifiably languishing under the loss of wife and child and good health, but his conversation, though not sprightly like James Russell's, is cheerful and a good deal more rational.

At supper Mrs Woodstock dominated, as she always does at such gatherings. There was an awkward moment when Mrs West, from ignorance, would have sat down at a table usually reserved for Mrs Woodstock and her party, but Mrs Holder swiftly removed her in time. However, our mother tells me that Mrs Woodstock had already given her a very sharp reproof when she (Mrs West) would have joined her table for vingt-et-un. I know that you have always maintained that Mrs Woodstock does indeed suffer from poor health, but I must say she appeared to be very robust and as disagreeable as ever to everyone except the Cravens.

"I see" she said sternly to me "that you were dancing with my husband's cousin, Miss Cowper."

"Yes ma'am," I replied. "Mr Rivers was obliging enough to ask me."

"I do not at all approve of Mr Rivers dancing. It is not suitable."

I did not ask if Mr Rivers' dancing was unsuitable because he was Mr Woodstock's cousin or because he was still deemed to be in mourning, and she went on, "I hear that your sister is still in Bath."

"Yes ma'am," I said, "she is accompanying my aunt and uncle who are taking the waters there."

"A great waste of time and money," she replied. "I never found the slightest benefit from them and Dr King has always said that those at Cheltenham are vastly superior. Do you know Cheltenham, Miss Cowper?"

"No, ma'am."

"I have always found it a very superior town," she continued, "quite different from Bath, which is sadly fallen off—full of fortune hunters and half-pay officers. Had I a daughter I would certainly not allow her to go to Bath, the company is scarcely what a conscientious mother would wish."

"My sister tells me" I said "that the Duchess of York and the Duke and Duchess of Clarence were at the last evening entertainment she attended."

But Mrs Woodstock appeared not to hear and turned towards Miss Craven to give her the benefit of her thoughts on the excellence of Cheltenham. Mr Woodstock seemed mortified at this evidence of his wife's rudeness and gave me his usual nervous smile. Poor man, one cannot but be sorry for him.

You will be interested to learn that the evening was notable for the first appearance of the new owner of Marshwood Abbey, Sir Edward Hampton. He too has lost his wife (though not recently) but looks very much more like one's idea of a widower, being tall and dark and melancholy looking, whereas Mr Rivers is fair-haired, of a slight build and of a cheerful countenance. Mrs Woodstock will have approved of Sir Edward for he did not dance, neither was he to be found in the card room. He stood at one end of the ballroom and spoke only to the more elderly gentlemen present—one wonders why he attended at all since I gather that his conversation was all of local business (our father tells us that he has been sworn Justice of the Peace in the room of old Mr Dewar) which could surely be better conducted in some other less frivolous place! Maria Brompton was moved to remark that he put her in mind of some Byronic hero, but, search as I might, I could see no sign of any such thing, which is just as well, since those are not the characteristics one would look for in someone engaged in the administration of the law. So you see what a lively time we had of it—I doubt of your having such a one in Bath!

Lucy is much concerned that her sister Sarah is so friendly with the Wests' maid Deborah, whom she categorises as a sly one—though upon what grounds I cannot say. It seems that Mistress Deb is forever in the kitchens at Holcombe Park and has thoroughly put poor Lucy's nose out of joint. I take it to be the novelty of a new face and someone who will listen to Sarah's woes about poor John coachman, for you will recollect that Lucy never thought him good enough for her sister in spite of his being a respectable young man and doting upon her.

I hope that your cough is gone and that you are otherwise well—and remain with love,

Yours affectionately,
E.C.

7th June

My Dear Charlotte,

I am very much obliged to you for writing to me again so soon; your letter yesterday was an unexpected pleasure. I am pleased that the fine weather has made such an improvement to your health that you were able to walk towards Twerton with Miss Irving and her brother, they are agreeable companions and he, especially, speaks a good deal of sense. I am sorry to hear that their father is no better, though, if, as you say, his habit has always been bilious, it may be too late for the waters to do him any good. Still, if the care of Mr Bowen has improved his spirits and appetite then that is some reason at least for coming to Bath.

If the cloak you speak of is still to be had I would be grateful if you will make the purchase for me, if, that is, the cost does not go beyond two guineas.

Everything is very flat here after the Ball and I shall be hard put to it to find anything to fill this paper. I greatly miss having you here at hand to talk over the events of the evening as we are wont to do. Indeed I would value your opinion of the new people who are come among us, since *your* judgement is more sound and sober than mine, which, as you have often had cause to remind me, is too satirical and partial!

Yet even you, I am persuaded, would approve of Mr Rivers. To have borne such sorrow and still remain rational and cheerful—and I do not think he is appreciated as he should be at Holcombe. Our mother said that she heard Mrs Woodstock addressing him in the most peremptory tones, commanding him to attend her the next day with a statement of the Barbados estate accounts (which one would, in any case, have thought should be left to Mr Woodstock) as she wished to examine them in *detail,* something it cannot have been easy for him to bear to hear shouted the length of the Assembly card-room! Mr Woodstock, you may be sure, was nowhere to be seen during this exchange, having learnt by long experience the embarrassment his wife is capable of causing in public places. Mr James Russell, however, was apparently present and, so our mother says, seemed much mortified by his aunt's behaviour. Mrs Woodstock was also heard (by me) to speak in very strong terms against poor Mr Wilmot and his Evangelicanism.

Our father tells me that he has invited Sir Edward Hampton to dine with us this week, together with the Chamberlynes, the Lythams (who it is hoped may have further news of William) and Mr Rivers. Our mother, from some misguided motive of kindness, has also invited Mrs West and her daughter, so I will have much to tell you in my next letter! Meanwhile, because of this, our mother desires that I break off now and consult with Cook to see if any fresh soles may be procured to go with the saddle of mutton, and what side dishes must be prepared—you can imagine with what fervour I wish you were here to attend to such tasks.

Your affectionate sister,
E.C.

My Dear Charlotte,

I have amazing news to relate. Mrs Woodstock is no more. She breathed her last yesterday and the whole of Lyme and the whole country from Taunton in the north to Seaton in the west echoes with the news and even the account I was to have given you of our dinner party yesterday is quite superseded.

You will say that you always believed Mrs Woodstock to be sickly and that now you are proved right, but, indeed, she died so suddenly and for no cause which is immediately discernible, that it cannot have been any of the complaints we have been so familiar with over the years that actually carried her off. For it seems she died quite peacefully in her sleep. I am obliged to Lucy for my immediate information—she tells me that Mrs Woodstock's maid Chapman, going in this morning to rouse her mistress, was unable to wake her and called Mr Russell, who at once summoned Dr King who pronounced life to be extinct. He declared that his patient's heart had failed, which I believe to be true, since most of us die when our hearts cease to beat! More than that I cannot tell you at present.

Certainly in Lyme opinion of Mrs Woodstock has already undergone a remarkable change—from being a monster of disagreeableness she is immediately transformed by death into a martyr to ill health whose unpleasantness and ill temper, everyone now agrees, was *quite* understandable given the pain she no doubt had to bear, poor soul, over the years. How Mr Woodstock will miss her, how her grieving nephew will mourn!

It will make a vast change to life at Holcombe, that is certain, and I sincerely pity Miss Craven, for I do not think that Mr Russell will offer for her now. That young man is free at last to follow his own inclinations, since, with a wife no longer there to tell him what he should do, Mr Woodstock will be a man easily guided. There—do not say that I have no news of any moment to fill my page!

To less remarkable matters. Our dinner party which, it now seems, was taking place while Mrs Woodstock was breathing her last, was most agreeable (Cook has mastered your recipe for scalloped oysters very well) and, in spite of an unpromising mixture of guests, might be deemed a success.

31

Knowing full well the impossibility of competing with Miss West's beauty, I decided only the smartest of gowns would do, so I took the liberty of borrowing your ivory lace overdress to make elegant my rose satin petticoat (the one with the seed pearl decoration). I do hope you agree that the occasion demanded this ruthless treatment of your property! I was glad that I had done so since Miss West was indeed a picture of loveliness in the most delicate of sprigged muslins with blue ribbon decoration. Her youth and bloom (illness notwithstanding) made the simplicity of her gown all the more appealing and most of the gentlemen (young and old) found themselves, at some moment, drawn towards her, and after dinner several of them did not linger long over the table but came in with the tea tray.

I spoke a little with Sir Edward Hampton but he is a severe-sounding man, very reserved and stiff, with an abrupt manner, so I found him difficult to converse with.

"Have you now settled into Marshwood Abbey, Sir Edward?" I enquired.

"My housekeeper complains that the kitchens are inconvenient, my groom is discontented with the stables, and, since my brother had no children the nurseries are less than adequate. Otherwise I have no problems."

"Did you bring your bailiff from Hatch Beauchamp to manage the estate?" enquired our father, who came up at that moment. "Will it answer do you think, or will local prejudice be too strong?"

Sir Edward, obviously grateful to have rational male conversation, thankfully turned in his direction and they were shortly engaged in the planning of a drain and the disposition of a field of barley.

You will recall that Sir Edward inherited the Abbey quite unexpectedly from his older brother who was unmarried and died earlier this year in a carriage accident, so I suppose it will take him some time to accustom himself to a larger estate than the one he had in Somersetshire. There are two little boys, and I do hope their father is more unbending with *them* or, lacking as they do a loving mama, their lives will be sadly oppressed.

You may imagine with what relief I turned to Mr Rivers, who was at his most conversable, not only full of pleasing anecdotes of his life in Barbados, but asking with real interest about the countryside hereabouts and the lives of the families who live here. You were wrong, in your last letter, to accuse me of having a *partiality* for him. Indeed I scarcely know him, but you must admit that it is a wonderful novelty to find a gentleman who at least gives the appearance of being interested in one's own affairs, however trivial, and is perfectly able to join in those flights of fancy that you know I like to indulge in. Were I indeed to have set my cap at him I should have a formidable rival in Miss West. Mr Rivers is too much a gentleman to allow his eyes to wander while he was speaking with one; still, I could not but notice that his gaze rested frequently upon her and he engaged her in conversation at the earliest moment he could politely leave me. But, alas, Mrs West remained at her daughter's side and conducted most of her conversation for her.

"And have you been able to explore the countryside, Miss West?" he asked. "It is very fine, is it not?"

"We have scarcely ventured far from Lyme as yet, sir," Mrs West replied, "though Miss Cowper and Miss Brompton have had the kindness to walk with Caroline in the immediate neighbourhood."

Miss West gave a small murmur of acquiescence and apparently encouraged by this, Mr Rivers continued, "Will your visit to Lyme be for some months?"

Miss West turned to her mama as if she too would like an answer to this question.

"It is not yet decided how long we will remain" Mrs West replied. "My daughter's health, as you must know, has not been good and we will remain here until she has quite recovered."

"I believe that you, too, have suffered ill health recently?" Miss West ventured.

Mr Rivers coloured with pleasure at this interest in his welfare. "I had the misfortune to take a fever in Barbados, but the kind air of Dorset has speeded my recovery," he said with a smile. Had he been Mr Russell he would no doubt have added a remark about the healing properties of pleasant company, but Mr Rivers (as I think I have mentioned already) does not flirt.

The Chamberlynes asked after you most kindly and she was loud in her lamentations that you are to go to Robert and Mary without returning home in July, sentiments with which I find myself in perfect accord! Mrs Chamberlyne also asked me to tell you that Mrs Harriot has had one fainting fit recently; it came on as usual after eating a hearty dinner but she says Dr King does not think there is any danger.

Perhaps Mrs Woodstock overate last night. I have no doubt I will be able to provide you with all the details you will certainly desire, since Lucy is to visit her sister tomorrow and will certainly bring back a budget of news.

I can recollect nothing more to say; when my letter is gone, I suppose I shall.

Yours affectionately,
E.C.

My Dear Charlotte,

I was very sorry to learn that my news of Mrs Woodstock's demise brought about a return of your palpitations, but relieved to hear that your taking hartshorn had a beneficial effect.

The neighbourhood has recovered from the novelty of her death and the talk is of how Mr Woodstock will attend to his affairs now that his wife is no longer here to manage them for him. The money, of course, is all Mrs Woodstock's, Mr Woodstock bringing only sadly neglected estates and himself to the match. Time and Mrs Woodstock's fortune have greatly improved the former but the latter (a poor thing, I imagine, even five and twenty years ago) has sadly declined, as we all must, with age.

Our father was at the funeral yesterday and said that poor Dr Matlock made a sad muddle of the service. Perhaps now that his wife is no longer able to overrule him, Mr Woodstock may be able to offer the living to Mr Wilmot when Dr Matlock resigns it, which event cannot be far off now.

Since you require me to do so, I offer you the account of Mrs Woodstock's passing that Lucy brought back from Holcombe Park—though I would beg you to keep the hartshorn within reach in case my narrative prove too much for you. It would seem that Mrs Woodstock was in perfect health all that day and in the morning went out in her carriage to visit Mrs Craven, taking Mr Russell with her, and was consequently in spirits, since she doubtless felt she had advanced that affair considerably. She was also greatly refreshed by an encounter with Mr Wilmot, who called to beg Mr Woodstock's help for one of his parishioners, Will Buller, who works in the gardens at Holcombe, and whose wife has recently died leaving him with five children all under eight years of age. The poor wretch was asking for some days' absence from his work so that he might look after the children until his sister could come down from Derbyshire to help him. It was a pathetic story which would have moved the stoniest heart and Mr Wilmot, I believe, pleaded his case with some eloquence. Alas, that was poor Will's undoing for Mrs Woodstock was present during the interview and, such is her aversion to Mr Wilmot, that she would by no means allow her husband to grant the poor man's request, saying that the children must go to the parish if their father could not care for them.

Invigorated by this skirmish, she dined with her husband and Mr Russell (Mr Rivers, as you will recall, dined with us) and her appetite was good—indeed she graciously praised the fricassee of chicken and asparagus (Sarah has given Lucy the receipt for this), something which, as you may imagine, is rare with her!

After dinner she required Mr Russell to play bezique with her for a while, but quite early on she complained of being tired and retired before her usual hour. Her maid Chapman took up her posset of wine and the laudanum she always takes each evening, and that was the last time that anyone saw her alive. The next morning, Sarah says, when Chapman went to wake her mistress, she could not rouse her and, as I have already told you, Dr King was sent for and life was pronounced extinct. We have not seen any of the Holcombe household, though, of course, our father did see them at the funeral. What a change there will be in all their lives. Mr Woodstock, for one will hardly know what to do with his freedom. Perhaps he may marry again (if his first experience of the state has not given him a dislike of it) or make the tour through Europe, or even return with his cousin to the West Indies—indeed, the world is open to him should he choose to explore it. Mr Russell must expect to have at least a half share of his aunt's fortune, which will give him his independence at last and freedom to pursue his own path in life and, indeed, in matrimony.

Our father, who had some conversation with Mr Rivers when he dined here, tells us that the poor man was much constrained in running the Barbados estate by constant commands from Mrs Woodstock, for although the property belonged to her husband, it was her money (as well as Mr Rivers' good management) that enabled it to flourish. Now it will be possible for him to order affairs there in his own way and the dignity of his position will at last be confirmed.

Perhaps even John coachman may hope to be reinstated and he and Sarah married at last. I cannot but think what a degree of felicity may arise from the death of one disagreeable old woman, though you may scold me for such an uncharitable thought!

Our mother prays that you will say everything kind for us to our aunt and uncle. She has taken to glove-knitting and every evening is filled with this activity. She requires me to ask what colour you desire so that she may make a pair for you.

Your visiting poor Lady Gordon was highly approved by everyone and applauded as an act of virtue on your part. I fear that what friends she may not have driven away by her ill humour will be even less inclined to visit her now that her health and her circumstances are both in such a bad way.

I shall take my olive drab cloak for the lining to be renewed and shall send yours that you left here on the chance of doing the same for you, though I believe your pelisse is in better repair than mine. Do not forget to write to Mary, she complains to me that she is neglected!

Yours affectionately,
E.C.

My Dear Charlotte,

Do not be angry with me for beginning another letter to you so soon, before I have one of yours to reply to, but I have mended my petticoat and read "The Corsair" and have nothing else to do. Getting out is impossible since there was a positive cloudburst this morning and the roads are too dirty for even such a desperate walker as I am.

Yesterday, though, I did go forth to make various purchases for our mother at Layton's where I spent all my money, and what is worse for you I have been spending yours as well. I went in for some checked muslin, for which I was obliged to give seven shillings a yard, but I was also tempted by a pretty coloured muslin and bought 10 yards of it, on the chance of your liking it—but, should it not suit you, you must not think yourself obliged to take it. It is only 3s6d per yard and I should not in the least mind keeping the whole. The pattern is a small green spot and the texture is just what we prefer. I got some bugle trimming for our mother at 2s4d a yard and three pairs of silk stockings at a little less than 12s the pair!

On my way back whom should I meet but Mr Russell. I was reluctant to speak with him, for you know how awkward it is to commiserate with someone on the death of a relative who was not much loved. But, although I turned my head as if I had not seen him, he came up and greeted me in such a loud and cheerful voice that I had no choice but to stop and be civil.

"My dear Miss Cowper," he said, "how pleased I am to come upon you like this. I was in such a state, overwhelmed by the gloom and tedium at Holcombe—you may imagine how melancholy things are—that I felt I had to break away and seek a livelier air and brighter company. And here you are, like a sign from heaven that the sun will not forever hide its face behind the clouds. Pray do me the greatest favour and walk with me for a while along the Cobb. The fresh sea air and your invigorating company are the two things I need most in the world!"

I was somewhat taken aback by the impetuousness of his address, but upon reflection I could perfectly well imagine how dull and depressing Holcombe Hall must be at present to one who has nothing particular to occupy him. Men, if they are away from home where they might be occupied with their own business and affairs, must find the time hangs heavy, since they cannot at such times fill their days with shooting, fishing or other outdoor occupations and such solaces as we women may have, as needlework, music or small domestic tasks, are denied them. I therefore decided that it was no more than my duty to relieve Mr Russell's boredom by walking with him beside the sea.

"We were all sorry to hear of your sad loss," I said formally, "and so unexpected too."

"As for that," he replied, "you know that my aunt's health has always been indifferent so that her death was not perhaps totally unexpected."

I was surprised by this statement, since in one of our previous conversations Mr Russell had implied what has been the general opinion, viz—that Mrs Woodstock's ill health was largely governed by whether or not she had her own way! Presumably now that she is dead she is to be allowed even by him to have suffered prodigiously in her lifetime.

"Indeed, sir," I said, "We have often heard that to be the case." He looked at me sharply, undecided whether I were being satirical or no, and I continued, "However, expected or not, death always comes as something of a shock, does it not?"

"That is very true," he responded quickly. "We have all been greatly shaken by the event."

"Has Dr King been able to determine the cause of death?" I enquired. He looked somewhat surprised at my question, having lived mostly in London and not knowing, I suppose, with what interest such things are regarded in a small community like ours.

"As to that," he replied, "the suddenness of her death—she was in good health and spirits the previous evening—makes it seem most likely that my aunt suffered an angina and that is Dr King's opinion."

"You must be happy that she went peacefully, in her sleep," I said.

"Indeed," he said warmly. "What is it Thomson says?
 Till loosen'd life, at last but breathing clay,
 Without one pang is glad to fall away."
We walked along in silence for some minutes, looking at the small boats tied up in the harbour. "What a delightful prospect this is," he said. "How much more pleasant than the dusty streets and hurly burly of London! How I wish I could stay in this spot for ever!"

"Do you return to London soon?"

"That I do not know at present," he replied. "My movements are uncertain, I must see how things are disposed, you will understand. I may not yet venture upon expectation. There is much that I would wish to do, much that I would wish to say, but I must be patient."

We returned along the Cobb and, as he offered me his arm to step down the slope, Maria Brompton came into view in company with Mrs West and her daughter. Mr Russell checked himself for a moment and said hastily, "Let us take the upper road, Miss Cowper. I fancy I see Miss Brompton and I do not feel able to face the endless comment and enquiry that will, I have no doubt, be forthcoming."

He escorted me back to our very gate, nobly carrying the parcel of muslin, but would not come in.

"If you will forgive me, I will continue my walk. Having had a taste of the healing powers of Nature I wish to continue the cure!" He bowed. "My thanks, ma'am, for your company and conversation."

While I must commend his gentlemanlike manner and his affability, I must confess that, after a short while I find Mr Russell's conversation insipid. There is, certainly a kind of high spirits and vivacity but I do not feel that there is any real depth of feeling or intelligence, nor, indeed, any humour. It may be that now, secure in his aunt's estate, and with proper occupation, he will develop those qualities, but I fear there may be a weakness of character which will forbid them.

It has come on to rain once more and I begin to fear that it will never be fine again. This is a finesse of mine, for I have often observed that if one writes about the weather, it is generally quite changed before the letter is completed.

41

I hope Miss Bennett is quite well again and had a comfortable dinner with you all. Does she remain as silent as ever? I recall, from my own last visit to Bath, the way she holds up her head and smiles and says nothing.

Lucy has just come in with several pairs of sheets to see which must be darned and which stitched down the middle. You can imagine how I wish you were here to give judgement on such weighty matters instead of me!

I had intended closing this letter after my talk with Lucy, but something most extraordinary occurred which I long to tell you about, so I will extend the letter well beyond its natural length and will have to write my lines very close together to get in all I wish to say! As I said, I laid my letter to one side to deal with household matters and was not able to take it up again yesterday. I had just settled myself in the back parlour after breakfast, meaning to finish writing to you, when Miss West was announced. She was looking, as usual, most handsome in a lilac walking dress and a straw bonnet lined with silk in a matching colour—you may imagine how delightful it looked. She seemed to have something on her mind other than the usual civilities of a morning call and she declined my offer of refreshment abstractedly and answered my remarks somewhat at random, often remaining silent and leaving me to continue the conversation as best I could.

"It is a great blessing, is it not," I persevered, "that the rain has finally stopped and the roads are passable for walking once more."

"Indeed," she said, "that is very true."

There was another silence and I began to wonder why she had come. Perhaps her mother had thought it politic that she should be on friendly terms with the more established families hereabouts, though she, herself, seemed to have no particular wish to pursue the acquaintance at this time. Certainly, after the eager, artless flow of Miss West's conversation on previous occasions I found this lack of communication strange indeed.

I allowed the silence to develop, hoping that the thought of us both sitting quite silent must eventually bring her to the point of saying something.

"Miss Cowper," she said after a while, "do you know Mr Woodstock well?"

The amazement I felt at such a question must have shown in my face, for she went on, "You must think my question an odd one, I daresay, but I have a particular reason for asking."

"Mr Woodstock," I replied cautiously, "has always seemed to me an amiable man."

"I am sure you will think it very strange of me to be inquiring of him in such a way," she went on in some confusion. "I hope you will not think it impertinent of me to be making such inquiries of you. But you have been acquainted with the family for many years and I have scarcely spoken to him and—well, there are reasons why I need to ask you..." She broke off as if she could not bring herself to continue.

As you may imagine, My Dear Charlotte, I was by now burning with curiosity to know her reason for this questioning.

"I have, as you say, known Mr Woodstock all my life," I said, "but I would not venture to say that I could describe his character in any depth since, as you will no doubt have heard mentioned by all who knew him, he lived very much in the shadow of his wife."

I regarded her keenly as I spoke, but she sat with her head cast down so that her face was shaded by her bonnet and I could not see her countenance.

After a moment she raised her head and looking at me with a candid gaze said, "I do most sincerely wish for your good opinion, Miss Cowper, and I am sure that I need not have the smallest fear of trusting *you*. Indeed, I should be most glad of your advice on how to manage in what is truly a most difficult position."

"Pray, Miss West," I said, "do not confide in me anything that you should not."

"No," she said firmly, "Mama said that you should be told of the situation, since she seemed to think..." She broke off in confusion, paused for a moment, and then went on more composedly, "I would like you to know our secret. I am engaged to Mr James Russell."

You may imagine my astonishment at this announcement, made bashfully, but with a sidelong look to see how I had taken it. You will appreciate, My Dear Charlotte, how astonished I was by this information. And yet, as I took it in, many things fell into place—the Wests' arrival in Lyme "for the sea air" and the reluctance of Mr Russell and Miss West to do more than exchange the merest civilities in public. Since Miss West, though blessed by Nature with a disproportionate amount of beauty, appears to have neither family nor fortune to recommend her, I have no doubt that Mrs. Woodstock would have been implacably opposed to such a match and it is obvious why the engagement had to be kept secret.

"Please accept my felicitations," I said at last. "I must confess that I am amazed at what you have told me—Mr Russell never spoke of you...."

Miss West coloured. "There were circumstances," she said hesitantly. "You will know that James is wholly dependent upon his aunt and she had—well, other plans for him."

Poor Miss Craven! Her case is hopeless indeed.

"And," Miss West continued, even more reluctantly, her hands fidgeting with the silk fringe of her purse, "even now we cannot make any public announcement of our engagement until we see how things are left...."

"Well," I said, "your secret is safe with me. But, forgive me if I express some surprise at your telling me. You must have felt that my being acquainted with it would hardly add to its safety."

Miss West bowed her head once more and spoke so quietly that I could scarcely hear her. "We thought," she said, "that is, Mama thought that you, yourself, not knowing of a previous arrangement, might have misunderstood how things stand..."

I remembered that Mrs West and her daughter had seen me walking with Mr Russell, had seen him give me his arm to step down from the Cobb. It would appear that Mrs West thought that I was trying to flirt with him and was warning me off! I must tell you, My Dear Charlotte, I did not know whether to be offended that she should think I would consider such a one as Mr Russell in that light, or to burst out laughing. I rose from my chair and paced about the room.

"Mr dear Miss West," I said coolly, "I have only the slightest acquaintance with Mr. Russell. He has not been so constant a visitor to the neighbourhood as might have made a friendship between him and any members of my family possible."

She blushed deeply and I felt momentarily sorry for her. Her position had been, and perhaps still is, a difficult one.

"Have you known Mr Russell long?" I asked in a more sympathetic tone.

45

"Indeed, for two years now. He was visiting a friend in Kent—Sir Richard Barton. My father, until he died last year, was Sir Richard's man of business. James and I met at an assembly in Tonbridge and we—we became acquainted."

One can imagine, can one not, how the attention of a young man like Mr Russell might well have been caught by Miss West's beauty, which was, no doubt, enhanced by the lack of any real competition in such a circumscribed society.

"He visited Kent as often as he could." Miss West's tone had now assumed something of its former vivacity now that the actual message had been given. "And when he was in London we corresponded." She caught my look of surprise and said defensively, "Mama knew that we had become engaged, we had her permission."

I could well imagine that Mrs West was delighted at such a match for her daughter, especially since her circumstances would have been even less comfortable after her husband's death.

"Did your father live long enough to hear of your engagement?" I asked. Miss West looked confused again and muttered something about nothing having reached that state while he was still alive, so I assumed that Mrs West had kept her own counsel about the affair, knowing that her husband would not have countenanced a secret understanding. Indeed, it would have been most awkward for him in his business dealings if such a thing had been made known to Mr Russell's friend Sir Richard, who would surely have been aware of Mrs. Woodstock's severe attitude to such an entanglement.

"What made you come to Lyme," I asked curiously.

Miss West smoothed the fringe on her purse again and said, "I had not been well—I was quite melancholy as you can imagine, at being separated for so long from James—and the doctor recommended sea air and a change of scene, so Mama thought that perhaps we should come down here. We had no expectation of seeing James here—I had thought that he was still in London—but Mama felt that if we might become acquainted with Mrs Woodstock we would know more clearly how she felt about our attachment."

46

I almost pitied Mrs West in her naive assumption that Mrs Woodstock might be persuaded to take a fancy to Miss Caroline and consider her a match for her nephew simply on the strength of beauty and pretty manners.

"But," Miss West said sadly, "even if James had not been here, we would have found it difficult to make the acquaintance of Mrs Woodstock, since, even at the Assembly, she seemed to speak only to her own circle." I remembered the reproof that Mrs Woodstock had given to Mrs West when that unfortunate lady tried to join her table in the card-room.

"She did for the most part," I said, "restrict her conversation to a very small circle of friends and acquaintances." It was obvious that the Wests had no more hope of forming an acquaintance with Mrs. Woodstock than with the Prince of Wales himself—less, indeed, since he has notoriously an eye for a pretty female!

"James was not pleased that we had come to Lyme," Miss West said. I could imagine his surprise and I must confess that I felt no little amusement at what must have been his nervousness. With Miss West on the one hand, supported by her Mama, and Miss Craven, on the other, urged on by his aunt, he was indeed caught between a veritable Scylla and Charybdis!

"So you see," Miss West said after a few moments silence, "you see why I wondered what manner of man Mr Woodstock is. I do not know if James will have his own inheritance or if, as Mama fears—that is, thinks—the property will be left to Mr Woodstock for his lifetime. If this is the case, do you think he will raise any objections to our marriage?"

She looked up at me, her large blue eyes dark as violets and I thought that if she regarded Mr Woodstock thus she need have no fear of his disapprobation.

"My dear Miss West," I said, "I really cannot venture to say *what* Mr Woodstock may feel on that score. However," I continued, "I imagine he will be more favourably disposed than his wife would have been."

That seemed to satisfy her for shortly after she took her leave. So you see, my dear, what astonishing circumstances I had to relate—well worth an extra 6d, I think! I shall watch

47

with great interest to see how Mr Russell behaves towards the Wests in future. No wonder he wished to avoid them when we came upon them by chance yesterday. Will he marry her, do you think? Does he truly love her, or was his aunt's disapproval merely an excuse for a flirtation he had no intention of taking seriously? It is obvious that Mrs West has taken it seriously enough, and I do not think that she would be easy to shake off. It seemed to me that, under that toad-eating exterior, lies hard steel! My hand aches with all this writing, so adieu.

Your affectionate and amazed sister,
E.C.

My Dear Charlotte,

You were mistaken in supposing I should expect your letter on Sunday; I had no idea of hearing from you before Tuesday and my pleasure yesterday was therefore unhurt by any previous disappointment. I was glad to hear that our uncle was better than he has been and is to bathe tomorrow and try the Electricity on Wednesday. Since he proposed the latter himself to Dr Fellowes, who made no objection to it, I can well believe that you and my aunt are unanimous in expecting no advantage from it.

You will be surprised to learn that Mrs Woodstock's brother, Sir Matthew Russell, has arrived. I saw him yesterday when I went with our father to pay a call on Mr Woodstock; our mother not feeling too stout and wishing to keep quiet was unable to join us. He is a cold, gentleman-like man, and although he was perfectly civil it was plain that he considered the company inferior to that which he is accustomed to. He is, as you may remember, a medical man of the very highest order and he explained that he had wished to come to his sister's funeral but, since he had been in attendance on the Duke of York at Bushey—a slight indisposition, but the Duke would have no other physician—it was obviously impossible for him to do so.

We all made suitable noises of assent, though I do not believe that the Duke would not (if asked) have spared him for such an occasion. However, Sir Matthew seemed so convinced of his own indispensability that I do not think anyone was inclined to disagree with him.

"I was greatly shocked," he said "to learn of my sister's death. When last I saw her she was in the best of health and I do not know of any reason why she should not have lived these next twenty years."

Mr Woodstock hastily replied that the death had been very sudden and that Dr King had been called immediately it was discovered. Sir Matthew announced his intention of questioning Dr King thoroughly about the matter, and indeed, I pity the poor doctor—the most conscientious and agreeable of men, as we all know—if he is to be put through such an examination!

When I told our mother about it when we returned (her head being better from a liberal application of the Steele's Lavender Water you sent her from Bath) she was very indignant on Dr King's behalf. She said that she had always thought Sir Matthew a most unpleasant man and had never been able to decide in her own mind whether he or his sister were the most tiresome. It was very sad, she said that the only agreeable member of that family, Mr James Russell's father Thomas, a military man, had died of a fever in Spain.

You tell me that Mr and Mrs Cosway are in Bath, lodging at the Charitable Repository—I wish the scene may suggest to Mrs C. the notion of selling her black beaver bonnet for the relief of the poor.

Mary complains that it is many weeks since she heard from you but says you are doubtless so immersed in the pleasures of Bath that you have no time to write, although she did tell you in her last that she has had one of her bad throats this last month or more and, as we are aware, her throats are always worse than anyone's. However, *I* remain your affectionate sister,

E.C.

My Dear Charlotte,

You will, I imagine, be surprised to receive another letter from me so hard upon my last, but I am just returned from another visit to Mr Woodstock and feel I must take up my pen at once to acquaint you with the latest news. I went with our mother who wished very much to learn for herself the result of Sir Matthew's cross-examination of Dr King.

"For you may depend upon it," she said as we sat in the carriage on the way to Holcombe Park, "he will have bullied the poor man quite dreadfully and goodness knows what he may have obliged him to say!"

We arrived to find Mr Woodstock in a state of great agitation and for a little while he was unable to find coherent words to tell us what had occurred. Fortunately Mr James Russell was present and was able to tell us that Sir Matthew was not satisfied about his sister's death and had actually announced that, in his opinion, the circumstances were doubtful. Indeed Sir Matthew was at this moment in the Library writing to some other eminent medical man whose opinion he wished for on the matter.

"But surely," our mother said, "he is not doubting Dr King's judgement in this? We all know that Dr King is an excellent physician. Why when Mary had that putrid throat as a child he brought her back from the very brink of the grave!"

On Sir Matthew's entering the room she continued upon this theme with considerable enthusiasm. Sir Matthew seemed unmoved by this tribute to a lesser member of his profession and spoke gravely of possible negligence or, at the least, inadequate examination of the body.

At this word Mr Woodstock became even more agitated and Mr Russell was obliged to ring for brandy to calm him.

"It is the greatest possible pity," Sir Matthew said "that I was not here when it happened. Now it may be necessary to obtain an exhumation order." At this I thought that Mr Woodstock was about to have a fit, causing Mr Russell to remonstrate with his uncle, who, finally becoming aware of his brother-in-law's distress, spoke more moderately.

"Dr King," he said in his patronising way, "appears to think that my sister died of an angina. That is certainly not the case. Had her heart been in any way affected I would, myself, it goes without saying, have been aware of the fact. Too many of these country physicians—if so they can be called—are inclined to attribute any death they are uncertain of to this cause. Of course," he continued in what I imagine he intended to be a conciliatory tone towards my mother, "they do not have the knowledge or experience to make any more reasoned judgements and one would not expect them to do so."

Our mother began to expatiate indignantly on Dr King's behalf with several anecdotes of his remarkable prescience in cases known to her, but Sir Matthew, who is, I am sure, not used to any sort of interruption or contrary view to his own, went on, "I intend to question the servants most closely as to the circumstances of my poor sister's last evening—what she ate and drank, for instance—and draw what conclusions I can from the consequences."

Mr Woodstock, seeing as a result of these cross-examinations, the end of all comfort in his house, protested that they had all been in his service for many years and were completely reliable, but he might as well have saved his breath. It was perfectly obvious that Sir Matthew was accustomed to taking charge, and since he, Mr Woodstock, had been unable to command his wife in anything, he was unlikely to be able to do anything to countermand anything her brother might wish to do!

As you can imagine, our mother spoke much of the matter on our way home. "Sir Matthew is the sort of man I detest. Mr King is worth ten of him. Now that tiresome man will stir up trouble and all to no avail—it will not bring back Mrs Woodstock and will distress poor Mr Woodstock, who, as anyone can see, is already quite distracted by all the fuss and nonsense."

I do agree with her sentiments entirely, wondering indeed whether even if the fuss could bring Mrs Woodstock back, we would altogether welcome her reappearance!

To more important matters. I would wish you to buy for me the brown cambric muslin that you spoke of (excellent for morning wear). Seven yards for my mother, seven and a half for me; a dark brown, but the kind of brown is left to your own choice and I would rather they were different, as it will always be something to say, to dispute about which is the prettiest.

Your affect. Sister,
E.C.

Yesterday I had the agreeable surprise of finding the scarlet strawberries quite ripe. There are more gooseberries and fewer currants than I thought at first—we must buy currants for our wine.

My Dear Charlotte,

All Lyme is now buzzing with the events at Holcombe Park. Mrs Woodstock's death has gone from being merely a great tragedy and is now become a powerful melodrama. Maria Brompton and Miss Gregory who called this morning to tell us of the possibility of an engagement between Elizabeth Finch and Mr Chute, Mr Fletcher's curate at Uplyme, were quite diverted from their purpose when our mother told them the latest news from Holcombe Park and willingly left poor Miss Finch in matrimonial limbo whence who knows if she will ever be rescued.

According to our Lucy, Sir Matthew has closely questioned Sarah and Chapman concerning the events of that fateful night, but Sarah was too frightened to do more than mumble very little and Chapman, who, as you know, is a sterner character altogether and almost as disagreeable as her late mistress, declined to do more than repeat what she had already told her master. So everything is at a standstill. This does not please Sir Matthew who is the sort of man who must be *doing* things so I daresay he will not let the matter rest. Meantime it does provide our circle with a prime subject for conversation now that the militia are removed from the neighbourhood. Speaking of which, I was much taken with your account of Lady Willoughby presenting the Colours to some Corps of Yeomanry in the Crescent, especially your description of her bonnet of cambric muslin—cambric being very much on my mind at present. You say they are a good deal worn and that some of them (though not Lady Willoughby's) are very pretty. However, I shall defer acquiring one of that sort until you are returned to advise me.

We have had an invitation from Sir Edward Hampton to dine at Marshwood Abbey. I do not expect much entertainment *there* since he seems to me, on the occasions I have met him, a melancholy man with no sort of conversation—or at least none which he is prepared to waste upon young women, being mainly occupied by agricultural and judicial matters (for on such he converses quite freely with our Father) and not willing to waste his time on female frivolities such as music, poetry and gossip. I will not, therefore, waste the delights of my new gown (muslin with a small red spot, made up for me last week by Mrs Ferris) upon the company, but will wear the plain white muslin—the one you advised me to dye blue, though I think I will not for the present—which is respectable without any pretension to *fashion,*which would, I feel, be out of place in that particular household.

We are like to have a great crop of Orleans plums, but not many greengages—on the standard hardly any, three or four dozen, perhaps, against the wall. Charming weather for us and I hope for you so that you may be able to take your walk with Miss Brydges. I will write after we have dined at Marshwood, though I do not have any expectation of there being much of interest to tell you of *that* visit.

Yr affect. Sister,
E.C.

My Dear Charlotte,

   I am pleased to say that my low expectations of our dinner party at Marshwood were not disappointed. It is a handsome house, I admit, but the furniture is sadly old fashioned and the want of any female touch means that there is an air of darkness and *gloom* about the place.

   The drawing room where we were entertained had many heavy pieces of ornate furniture that must, I believe, have belonged to Sir Edward's grandfather, and I wonder that his mother, the late Lady Hampton, suffered them to remain, which makes me think that she must have been a poor sort of woman, not much given to opinions of her own!

   The dinner itself was well prepared, even our father (who is, as you know, a self confessed expert on such things) admitted later that he had never tasted a finer saddle of mutton, and I was delighted to find a splendid selection of cakes and jellies, which made me think that Sir Edward was fortunate in his cook and his housekeeper. And, indeed, this proved to be the case for when the housekeeper herself brought in the tea tray after dinner while Sir Edward and our father were sitting over their port, she appeared to be a most sensible woman. Our mother—as you may imagine—questioned her closely and discovered to her pleasure that Mrs Hodges—for that is her name—is the sister of Tom Jennings who is a tenant of Mr Woodstock at Upper Bracklands farm near Holcombe. This immediately set the seal upon her respectability. She vouchsafed the information that Sir Edward was a good master and away from home a great deal—whether the one fact influenced the other I cannot tell. His being away so much, she said, was sad for the two little boys, whose governess Mrs Hodges declared to be an indifferent sort of person, scared of her own shadow and not at all suited to instruct and entertain two lively children. I think she would have said more but, upon the gentlemen entering the room, she very properly withdrew.

   The conversation was not particularly lively, for, although Sir Edward said everything that was suitable to our mother and to me, he seemed more inclined to continue the conversation he had been having with our father in the dining room—something tedious about shooting and the prospects for the coming season—and I felt his attentions to us were merely polite. For, as you know, no young lady will think favourably of a man who heaps praise upon his new gun dog while appearing impervious to *her* charms. Indeed, I wondered why he had not simply made a morning call upon our father instead of inviting us all to dine, and on our own with no other family to share the "entertainment."

However, he did know about William and his position on the *Scorpion* and, since he is a cousin of an Admiral of the White, he promised to make enquiries about William's present situation. This, of course, was enough to make our mother consider him the most excellent of men and I certainly felt more favourably disposed towards him in spite of the dullness of the evening.

In the carriage on the way home our mother said, "It was kind of Sir Edward to offer to get us news of William. But he does seem to be an odd sort of man and I must confess I was surprised to find no other company there but ourselves."

"He is but lately come into the neighbourhood," our father said, "and has made very few acquaintances as yet, having been away a great deal, and as a widower has no wife to make calls and receive them. The fact of his inheriting unexpectedly means that he has been consulting me, since I was a friend of his brother until his untimely death, as to certain details about the running of the estate. Our being the only guests tonight was, I believe, a mark of his respect and gratitude to me for the help I have been able to give him on the matter."

Our mother, who as you know, has never bothered herself about such things as estate management, merely repeated that it would still have been more comfortable with some other guests.

"And those poor little boys. So young! How sad for them to have lost their mama! I am sorry we did not see them. Mrs Hodges—a good sort of woman, Sir Edward is fortunate to have her—said that the governess was quite useless, and I would have liked to have seen for myself how matters stood. However, perhaps an opportunity may yet arise for me to do so."

"I am sure, my dear," our father said "you will manage to make such an opportunity."

Which reminds me to tell you how the new carriage is liked—very well indeed, except for the lining, but our father is pleased with it as is Will coachman, his approval being, perhaps, the more important.

I must hasten now to thank you for the stockings which I liked very much and greatly prefer having only two pairs of that quality to three of an inferior sort. The combs are very pretty and I am much obliged to you for your present; but am sorry you should make me so many.

We all unite in best Love and I am

Your very affect. Sister,
E.C.

My Dear Charlotte,

Such news! Sir Edward called especially to give our father a letter he had received from the Admiral about William. "He has been continued in the *Scorpion;* but I have mentioned to the Board of Admiralty his wish to be in a frigate and as it is judged that he has taken his turn in a small ship, I hope he will be removed. Indeed, I am glad I can give you assurance that his promotion is likely to take place very soon, as Lord Spencer has been so good as to say he would include him in an arrangement that he proposes making in a short time relative to some promotions in that quarter." You will imagine our delight at this! Our mother spoke again and again of our gratitude and our father said everything that was proper.

"It was nothing," Sir Edward said. "I was pleased to be able to repay in some small way the debt I owe to you sir, for the help you have given me regarding the estate." His manner is, as I have probably told you, very stiff, and it is difficult to engage him in ordinary conversation, but we certainly owe him a debt of gratitude for this favour. I long to see William and our father thinks it probable that the *Scorpion* may be come in soon for a refit and we may hope to have letters from him then.

Meanwhile our father and Sir Edward being then occupied with a discussion of cows, bacon, hay and hops, and other such agricultural matters I removed my attention and concentrated on designing in my head my new bonnet in which I plan to surprise the company at the picnic the Holders are planning for later next week. It is to be of straw—to suit the rustic nature of the party—with green ribbons and perhaps daisies and cornflowers to continue the theme. Do you not think it sounds charming and will be the cause of much admiration (and some jealousy)?

You will be pleased to learn that Maria Brompton's rug is finished at last—I saw it when I visited her yesterday—and it looks well, tho' not as well as she had hoped. There is no fault in the border, but the middle is dingy. She says she will not attempt another.

We hear from Lucy that Mr Wilmot, emboldened perhaps by the absence of his former adversary, called upon Mr Woodstock last week to plead the cause of John coachman, and it is now decided that he is to be re-instated. You may imagine the delight with which this news was received by Sarah, since the wedding may go ahead at last. She told Lucy that Mr Woodstock had given John 3*l* and said that they should have the cottage by the lodge gate at Holcombe. I do not know whether it be the effect of Mr Wilmot's warm words or Mr Woodstock's guilt at the unreasonable behaviour of his late wife but certainly the result is cause for much rejoicing. It may be that this is the time for Mr James Russell to put forward his own matrimonial plans for his uncle's approval. I believe Miss West (and certainly Mrs West) will expect him to do so.

Pray tell our Aunt that I cannot yet satisfy her as to Mrs Foote's baby's name, and I must not encourage her to expect a good one, as Captain Foote is a professed adversary to all but the plainest; he likes only Mary, Elizabeth, Anne &c. Our best chance is 'Catherine', which in compliment to his sister seems the only exception.

Our garden is putting in order by a Man who bears a remarkably good character, has a fine complexion and asks less than the first.

I hope your cough is gone and that you are otherwise well. And remain with love,

Yrs affectionately,
E.C.

My Dear Charlotte,

My expectation of having nothing to say to you after the conclusion of my last seems nearer truth than I thought it would be, for I have but little. There is one event, however, that has occasioned some pleasure and that is the departure of Sir Matthew to London. It seems, according to his own account, that the Duke of York has succumbed to a minor indisposition and will have no-one but Sir Matthew to attend him. This, of course, may be the fact of the matter, indeed I have every expectation of reading in the papers that the Duke is suffering from a slight cold, but whether he has expressed a positive wish for Sir Matthew's presence I am more doubtful.

Nevertheless the general feeling is that of relief at his departure. I am sure that is particularly true of poor Mr Woodstock, who has hardly yet recovered from Sir Matthew's declaration that Mrs Woodstock's death was suspicious. The general feeling in Lyme is that poor Dr King has been sadly traduced by Sir Matthew and everyone seems determined to show their support. Indeed I do believe that Dr and Mrs King have never, in all the years they have lived in Lyme, received so many invitations to dine. Some from motives of sympathy, and some, I daresay, from curiosity as to the final hours of Mrs Woodstock. Our mother's opinion is that Dr King is a much finer physician than Sir Matthew and that the Duke of York would be far better served by having him in attendance, citing Dr King's miraculous effect upon Mary's putrid throat.

I endeavour as far as I can to supply your place and be useful and keep things in order. The chickens are all alive and fit for the table, but we save them for something grand. This may be quite soon since our father has invited Sir Edward Hampton to dine with us. It is not yet decided who will be invited with him, my mother's suggestion of Dr and Mrs King was rejected by our father who says it would not be suitable.

It seems that before he left for London Sir Matthew Russell requested, nay demanded, that Sir Edward should investigate the circumstances of Mrs Woodstock's death. I gather that the latter was most reluctant to do so, declaring to my father that it was all a great deal of nonsense, but, given that he is but newly appointed magistrate and in consideration of Sir Matthew's connections in high places, he felt compelled to agree. I can quite understand why our father is reluctant to invite Sir Edward and Dr King together, but our mother is most indignant and says it is tantamount to accusing Dr King of I know not what. On our father's suggesting that Mr Russell and Mr Rivers might be of the party, she pointed out that they too might be considered unsuitable to be entertained at the same time as Sir Edward in his capacity of magistrate, and it seemed to her that if such considerations were to be acted upon then we will now be barred from inviting the greater part of our acquaintance to meet him. However, this interesting event—whoever may be invited—will not take place immediately since Sir Edward is gone into Somersetshire again on business and will not return within the next ten days.

To set against your new novel, of which nobody has ever heard before, and perhaps never may again, we have got "Ida of Athens," by Miss Owenson, which must be very clever, because it was written, as the authoress says, in three months.

There, I flatter myself I have constructed you a smartish letter, considering my want of materials; but, like my dear Dr Johnson, I believe I have dealt more in notions than in facts.

Yours affectionately,
E.C.

My Dear Charlotte,

You will be happy to learn that our father has this day received a letter from Frank in Vienna, sent with dispatches to Lord Keith. A great part of it was concerned with diplomatic matters and the progress of the mission, and our mother was disappointed that there was not more information about the various personages and descriptions of the court. However, I could not but reflect what a fine thing it is to have a brother who moves in diplomatic circles and is thus privy to the high secrets of state that lesser mortals must remain in ignorance of. He does not say how long he will remain there since it seems that negotiations are not progressing well.

What fine weather this is! Not very becoming perhaps early in the morning, but very pleasant out of doors at noon, and very wholesome—at least everybody fancies so, and imagination is everything. Since it was so fine yesterday I called upon Maria Brompton to suggest we might walk together as far as Uplyme. However, she was engaged to visit Layton's with Miss West who is anxious to purchase some rose-coloured satin to line a cloak, in which she no doubt wishes to dazzle Mr Russell. Maria suggested that I should join them, but, given the circumstances of my last meeting with Miss West, not to mention the fact that I find her company excessively tedious, I declined.

Being determined on a walk I took the path towards Marshwood, which because of the fine weather was quite dry underfoot. I had not progressed for more than half a mile when, rounding a bend, I was almost knocked off my feet by a hoop vigorously bowled by two small boys. They were much abashed by the incident and stood nervously waiting for some sort of rebuke. A young woman came up behind them and began to apologise profusely.

"I am so sorry ma'am, they ran on ahead of me and I could not keep up with them. I do hope you are not injured in any way..."

"There is no harm done, I assure you, I was merely startled." The boys still looked anxious, so I continued, "It is a very fine hoop, quite like the ones my brothers used to have and which they would never allow me to try."

They looked more hopeful at this and the older of the two offered me a turn with this one—which I was obliged reluctantly to decline. Their governess, for so I took her to be, was very shocked at this exchange and said she could not imagine what their father would say when he heard of it.

"Pray do not bother him with such a trifling matter," I said. "Am I right in thinking that these are the sons of Sir Edward Hampton? I am sure he has many other more important matters to consider than youthful high spirits."

"They are indeed the sons of Sir Edward..." the governess began when the older boy, who I took to be about ten years old, extended his hand and said "I am George Hampton, ma'am and this is my brother John and we are very sorry." I shook the proffered hand and said I was delighted to make his acquaintance. The governess, obviously wishing to bring the incident to a close, once more murmured some apologies, and, turning round led the boys back the way they had come. I too turned back and proceeded homeward. When I told our mother of my encounter she was full of sympathy for the boys and said it was a shame for them to be cooped up in that gloomy house with only a spiritless governess for company.

"To be sure William and Frank were often wild and boisterous at that age," she said "but that is the nature of boys and certainly no-one could have turned out as well or given us so much cause for satisfaction. But, there, with no mama and Sir Edward so busy with his own affairs I suppose they are bound to be neglected. Talking of Sir Edward," she went on "Mr Russell called while you were out and I am sure he is very put out that Sir Edward is to investigate his aunt's death. He did not say so in so many words, but it seemed to me that he considered it an impertinence on Sir Edward's part."

I said that was a little unfair since Sir Edward was only performing his duty as a magistrate and could hardly do otherwise, but our mother continues to regard the whole affair as a slight upon Dr King and cannot be moved from that position.

I have made myself two caps to wear in the evening and they save me a world of torment as to hair-dressing, which now gives me no trouble beyond washing and brushing, for my long hair is always plaited up out of sight, and my short hair curls well enough to want no papering.

I note what you say about not using the receipt for chicken and asparagus fricassee that Lucy procured from Sarah. I do not believe that it was in any way responsible for Mrs Woodstock's demise, since both her husband and her nephew both partook of it with no apparent ill effects. When I mentioned your misgivings to our mother, she declared that if it had been so Dr King would certainly have mentioned it. So that must be the final judgement on the matter. She continues to attribute Mrs Woodstock's death to ill temper and over indulgence in Madeira wine. Nevertheless, perhaps we should settle on having a plain roasted bird when Sir Edward comes to dine since any possible threat to a magistrate might put us in danger of the law.

Our mother said that Mr Russell looked remarkably well—legacies are a very wholesome diet and I am sure that being relieved of the threat of Mrs West's approaching his aunt with her story must add greatly to his well-being. However, I imagine this happy state of affairs cannot continue forever, for the lady is determined and Mr Russell may not yet be sure of his uncle's blessing to such an unequal match. You can imagine with what pleasurable anticipation I await the next development in the matter.

You deserve a longer letter than this; but it is my unhappy fate seldom to treat people so well as they deserve.

Yours affectionately,
E.C.

My Dear Charlotte,

You are quite mistaken in thinking that I am interested in Sir Edward and his family. It is true that I found his sons delightful and I am indeed sorry for their unhappy situation. But as for their father, he seems to me a singularly *uninteresting* man. I find that kind of stern countenance and general gravity most dispiriting, and when one does converse with him he takes little trouble to listen to what one has to say and answers as briefly as possible. As for your thinking him shy, I am sure that is no such matter, since he appears to have no trouble in talking quite animatedly to our father about estate and sporting matters. No, I fear he can only be set down as a *dull* man—as you know, my particular aversion—and I shall spend no more time talking of him.

Of my charities to the poor since you left you shall have a faithful account. I have given a pair of worsted stockings to Mary Hutchins, Dame Kew, Mary Stevens, and Dame Staples; a shift to Hannah Staples and a shawl to Betty Dawkins; amounting in all to about half a guinea.

You will be interested to know that Lucy has it from Sarah that Sir Edward called at Holcombe Park with the intention of carrying away the bottle containing the laudanum that Chapman was accustomed to administer to Mrs Woodstock every evening. As you may imagine, Chapman, not the easiest of servants, made a great fuss at this, crying out that she was being accused of murdering her mistress. Poor Mr Woodstock had a good deal of trouble to pacify her, being greatly upset himself, and only the continuing reassurances of Mr Rivers (Mr Russell being away from home) served to calm them both. I gather that Sir Edward merely stood by and watched this disturbance with some irritation and made no attempt to ameliorate it. This makes him unfeeling as well as dull, a combination which you must admit is past bearing.

I imagine he has taken the bottle away for examination to see if it does indeed contain laudanum and not a strange poison from some far-off land. Most exciting—we might well be living in a Gothick novel!

Our mother, as you may well imagine, considers Sir Edward's action to be yet another slight upon Dr King, and if it were not for the fact that invitations have already been given to Mr Rivers, Mr and Mrs Chamberlyne, the Holders, Maria Brompton, and Sir Edward himself, and that a whole salmon has been ordered, she would have been in favour of cancelling the affair.

You will have noted that Mr Russell was not invited, although his cousin is to make one of the party. He is gone to London, it is said 'on business,' but I wonder if it may not be to avoid any encounter with Mrs West, and she will surely not approach Mr Woodstock while he, Mr Russell, is absent. Mr Woodstock himself was sent an invitation to dine, it being thought that his period of mourning might not prevent his participating in so modest an entertainment, but he sent a message to say that his nerves were still too unsteady to permit his venturing out. It must be a novel experience for him to be able to claim any ailment of the nervous system, for that has been hitherto the sole prerogative of his wife.

Hancock has been here today putting in the fruit trees. A new plan has been suggested concerning the plantation of the new inclosure of the right-hand side the elm walk: the doubt had been whether it would be better to make a little orchard of it by planting apples, pears, and cherries, or whether it should be larch, mountain ash and acacia. What is your opinion? I say nothing and am ready to agree with anybody.

I have had many enquiries as to when you are coming back to Lyme and have had to explain that you are promised to Mary when you should leave Bath. I have just this day received a letter from Mary complaining that she had been expecting you this last week and declaring our uncle's attack of gout, which prevented this event, to be 'all imagination' and most inconvenient for her. However, I gather from your letter that you are to be conveyed thence by our uncle and aunt when they leave for London so you will have a more comfortable journey than if you had been obliged to travel by post. I imagine they will break their journey somewhere else on the road and *not* pass the night with Mary, Robert and the children, since I fear the latter, especially with a new addition to the family, would not be to our uncle's comfort even if he were in completely good health.

You will be amused to learn that Rugeley, as an inducement to our continued subscribing, insists that his collection is not to consist only of novels, but of every kind of literature, &c. He might have spared this protestation to *our* family, who are great novel-readers and not ashamed of being so; but it was necessary, I suppose, to the self-consequence of half his subscribers.

I will await impatiently an account of your journey and news of Mary.

Your affectionate sister,
E.C.

My Dear Charlotte,

I am very glad your journey was comfortable and that you found the roads in excellent order and had good horses all the way. I am sorry to hear that Mary had one of her headaches when you arrived and it was well that our uncle and aunt had arranged merely to drink tea and then proceed upon their journey.

I am happy to learn that little Charlie is grown and is a now a fine boy of six and that Anne has such charming ways. I am sure they are delighted to have their favourite aunt with them again. It is fortunate that our uncle's indisposition did not keep you any longer in Bath since the christening of the latest offspring is to be next week and your presence as his chief sponsor could not well be spared. Have they yet decided upon a name? I believe Mary favoured Percival while Robert stands firm by John, the name of his uncle with the East India Company from whom he has expectations.

I was fortunate enough to encounter Mr Rivers as I was walking along the Parade and he told me that Sir Edward, now back from Somersetshire, has called upon Mr Woodstock. This visit, as you may well imagine, after the upset of the last one, caused much alarm, Chapman going off into hysterics at the prospect of facing one she takes to be her accuser. However, all was well. Sir Edward returned the bottle and told Mr Woodstock that the contents were simply the mild tincture of laudanum that Mrs Woodstock had been accustomed to taking and that, even if more drops of it than usual had been administered, it would not have been sufficient to cause her death. Indeed he told Mr Rivers, who was also present, that had she taken the whole bottle, although the effects might have been unpleasant, it would not have been fatal.

"So," Mr Rivers asked (Mr Woodstock being much taken aback by this blunt remark), "do you mean that there is no reason to think that her death was anything but natural?" But apparently Sir Edward refused to commit himself on this score, saying that further enquiries were being made. This, of course, threw Mr Woodstock back into a state of agitation so that Mr Rivers had much ado to calm him. After a mere exchange of civilities Sir Edward took his leave without giving the poor man any sort of reassurance.

I exclaimed upon his lack of sensitivity in handling the affair and Mr Rivers said, "Sir Edward is a very good sort of man, most conscientious, and only doing his duty in this matter. As for his manner, he was a soldier before he came into his inheritance—that is the estate at Hatch Beauchamp, left to him, I believe, by an uncle—and soldiers, you know, are inclined to be abrupt."

"Indeed, sir, I had not heard he was a military man."

"He was on Wellington's staff for a while," Mr Rivers said, "and I believe the Duke thought highly of him." So I suppose we must excuse Sir Edward his manner since he learnt it from his commanding officer—I remember Frank saying that the Duke could often appear forbidding, though I believe he would unbend and was perfectly civil in the company of ladies!

So the mystery remains—if mystery indeed it is—as to what caused Mrs Woodstock's death, though the fact that Sir Edward continues to pursue the matter would seem to suggest that he still has doubts on that score. From our conversation, I was struck again by Mr Rivers's good sense and am pleased that Mr Woodstock has so sensible a relative to support him, especially since Mr James Russell has seen fit to absent himself at the time when he might be useful to his uncle. I do not know when he, Mr Rivers, intends to return to Barbados, but I believe he will remain as long as this unhappy business over Mrs Woodstock continues.

Our mother is very happy in the prospect of dressing a new doll for Anne as you requested and desires me to tell you that it will be despatched as soon as she has found materials enough to complete it. Our father is glad to hear so good an account of Robert's pigs, and desires he may be told, as an encouragement to his taste for them, that Lord Bolton is particularly curious in his pigs, has had pigstyes of a most elegant construction built for them, and visits them every morning as soon as he rises.

Remember me affectionately to everybody and believe me your affectionate sister E.C.

My Dear Charlotte,

Our dinner party has now taken place and may be considered a success. The salmon and the roast fowl were both excellent and the ragout of veal, in spite of my doubts on the matter, was perfectly good.

Sir Edward being of the company and Mr Woodstock being absent, the conversation, as you may imagine, largely turned upon the death of Mrs Woodstock. This was obviously not to Sir Edward's liking. His chief questioners, you will not be surprised to hear, were Mrs Holder and Maria Brompton who, in spite of the briefest and most unhelpful of replies, persisted in asking for details of the death and the progress of the investigation. Our mother was anxious to know Sir Edward's attitude to Dr King and was much gratified to learn that he roundly condemned Sir Matthew's treatment of him. Since he also let it be inferred that he considered Sir Matthew a pompous fool, our mother found herself completely in charity with him.

I was pleased to have some conversation with Mr Rivers, who tells me that Mr James Russell is expected back from London within the next week. It is to be hoped he will not immediately inform his uncle of his marriage plans—if such they be—since the poor man having barely recovered from the death of his wife and the subsequent upsets that followed it, will, I have no doubt, be thrown once again into a state of agitation by such a piece of news. Fortunately Mr Rivers is to remain in Lyme for the present, for, although Dr King has pronounced him fully recovered from the fever that brought him home from Barbados, he feels he may be of use and comfort to Mr Woodstock. He also confided in me that he now hopes to forward plans for the Barbados estate that Mrs Woodstock had dismissed.

"I do not believe," he said "that she had considered them closely, though I had laid out the plans in much detail with the possible advantages, both as to the immediate profit as well as the long term improvement of the estate. I hesitate to say this, but I fear Mrs Woodstock was not inclined to consider anything new, however beneficial it might be, if the proposal did not come from herself."

"But surely the estates belong to *Mr* Woodstock," I said. He permitted himself a brief smile and said, "I imagine you are aware of what the position there has been. But now," he continued "I have hopes of Mr Woodstock's agreeing to some, at least, of the plans I have suggested."

"Do you think that Mr James Russell will wish to be consulted?" I asked, mindful of the talk about his inheritance.

"Of course I believe that Mr Woodstock will wish to consult his nephew, but I am confident that Mr Russell will be happy with any suggestions that will improve the value and profit of the estate."

Certainly I must agree that Mr Russell is very conscious of such things as value and profit. But however it may be gained, I sincerely hope that Mr Rivers will achieve consent for his plan, since he appears to me to be a wholly estimable man, kind and considerate, and it seems hard that Mr Russell should have the benefit when he has done nothing to deserve it. But, as I am sure you will remind me, Life is not fair and we should not expect it to be otherwise.

I also had some words with Sir Edward. "The whole of Lyme, sir," I said, "is talking of the laudanum bottle you removed from Holcombe."

He looked annoyed at my re-introducing the subject he thought he had dealt with. "People seem," he said, "to have very little to do with their time but indulge in rumour and gossip."

"I believe poor Mr Woodstock was greatly upset at your last visit."

"I had hoped," he said irritably, "not to have troubled Mr Woodstock, who seems to be in a highly excitable state, but to have had a quiet word with Mr James Russell. But he had gone to London—on business they said, though what business he may have had that was more important than supporting his uncle at a difficult time I do not know. However," he continued, "I believe that young men of his sort will journey to London simply to have their hair cut fashionably."

"I believe that is so."

He looked at me suspiciously as if to see whether I was being satirical. "Fortunately, Mr Rivers was present and was able to quiet his cousin. He appears to be a very capable and sensible man."

"I believe he speaks in the highest terms of you."

He gave me the same suspicious look so I thought it better to stop provoking him (though it is tempting to do so since he rises to the bait so easily) and change the subject. "I had the pleasure, sir, of meeting your sons the other day."

His face lightened and he said "Ah, *you* were the mysterious lady they spoke of so warmly! Though Miss Blair, their governess, was afraid their behaviour distressed you."

"What nonsense!" I exclaimed. "They were charming boys and so well mannered—indeed they offered me a turn with their hoop, an invitation I would gladly have accepted but that I feared their governess would disapprove."

He smiled. "I am afraid they have long since outgrown a governess and should be in school, especially George, who is nearly ten years old. But, because of my situation, I have been reluctant to part them and have waited until John should be eight and able to go with his brother. They are to go to Winchester."

"My brothers were both at Winchester; I am sure they will be happy there. When do they go?"

"John will be eight years old next year."

"Sir Edward," I said on an impulse (something you have often had cause to reprove me for), "I wonder whether you would allow me to take your sons to collect fossils. It is something my brothers, my sister and I used to do when we were young. It is excellent sport and," I added, "also educational."

"Fossils?"

"Indeed Lyme is famous for them."

"I believe I read several years ago about an important find by a young girl."

"Yes, Mary Anning. It was her father who showed my brothers how to discover them. And our friend Miss Philpot and her sister, who are vastly knowledgeable in these matters, taught my brother Frank a great deal about them. He had a decided turn for scientific studies and might well have pursued that line if my uncle had not found a place for him in the diplomatic service."

Sir Edward was somewhat taken aback by all this information—as well he might be—but simply said, "That is very kind of you Miss Cowper, but I cannot believe you would wish to burden yourself with the activities of two small boys."

"On the contrary, it would give me great pleasure—searching for fossils was a great pastime of mine and, since it may not be considered suitable for a young woman on her own, your sons will be doing me a service if they give me the excuse of accompanying them."

He gave me a slight smile. "I that case, Miss Cowper, I will gladly give my permission."

So I am to send a note to Marshwood to say when I am free and their governess will bring them into Lyme for the expedition. You will, I fear, think it was very forward of me to make such a suggestion—I believe Sir Edward may have thought so—but I was so struck by the sad situation of the boys that, when the idea came to me, I could not help it. Our mother, who shares my sentiments in this matter, thoroughly approves and has commanded me to bring them back here to eat cakes after the expedition. I think she also wishes to inspect their governess.

Mrs Holder says she will be much obliged if you will send her daughter the pattern of the jacket and trousers, or whatever it is that Mary's boy wore when he was first put into breeches; if you could send an old suit itself, she would be very glad, but I suppose that is hardly done.

Love to all. I am glad little Charlie remembers me.

Your affectionate sister,
E.C.

My Dear Charlotte,

How do you do and how is Mary's cold? I trust that you have not taken it also. I hope Charlie was pleased with my designs. Tell him I will send him another picture when I write next. I suppose baby grows and improves. I fear Mary was not pleased that they settled on the name of John so I shall continue for the present to call him nothing but baby.

I was much struck by your observation that it is no wonder Sir Edward is still investigating Mrs Woodstock's death since there are so many who might profit by it. Indeed, this is nothing but the truth and deserves some consideration. We do not yet know how Mrs Woodstock has disposed of her property, but it seems likely that Mr James Russell will benefit from the uncle's indulgence now that he is no longer dependent on the whim of the aunt. It is also fortunate that, if Mrs West should reveal the secret engagement, he is less likely to face the consequent loss of favour and possible disinheritance, since I believe he would be quite able to bring his uncle round.

Of course it cannot be denied that Mr Woodstock himself will lead a happier life without his formidable spouse, though I do not believe that he could have summoned up the courage to dispose of her!

Mr Rivers will be glad to be rid of one who would have put obstacles in the way of his plans for the Barbados estate, but I do not think that may be considered a sufficient reason for an honourable man to take a life.

Mrs West, however, seems to me to lack such scruples if they stood in the way of her daughter's advancement. I do not at present see how she *could* have brought about Mrs Woodstock's demise, but no doubt, if I give my mind to it, I may presently think of something.

Poor John coachman also had reason to wish his mistress dead, since his whole happiness (and that of Sarah) depended upon keeping his position at Holcombe and if he had been turned away without a character his case would have been miserable indeed.

So you see, there are a number of people who will be happy at Mrs Woodstock's death. Perhaps I should add myself to the list for the sake of those hours of tedium and the many irritations she has subjected me to!

I have found your white mittens; they were folded up within my old nightcap, and send their duty to you.

I have arranged with Miss Blair, the Hampton children's governess, to take them fossil hunting tomorrow and, with that in mind, I have, with some difficulty, found the small hammers that Frank and William were wont to use for the purpose. They were in the large cupboard in the schoolroom, right at the back in an old box containing one ice skate (Frank), a copy of Herodotus with the cover torn off and ink drawings of ships and anchors in the margins (William), a half-completed sampler hidden away by me many years ago for fear Miss North might make me finish it, a copy of some Italian songs that none of us cared for and the book of pressed ferns that occupied so much of your time until you wearied of it and turned your attention to collecting riddles. I will let you know how our expedition fares.

Mr Peter Debary has declined the Dean curacy; he wishes to be settled near London. A foolish reason! As if Dean were not near London in comparison with Exeter or York. Take the whole world through, and he will find many more places at a greater distance from London than Dean. What does he think of Glencoe or Lake Katherine?

Our father thinks Dean might do very well for Mr Wilmot if Mr Woodstock does not offer him Westover now that Mrs Woodstock is no more. Now I come to think of it, perhaps I should add Mr Wilmot to the list of those likely to profit by Mrs Woodstock's death, though you will admonish me for suggesting such a motive for a clergyman even though he is an Evangelical.

I will not say that your mulberry trees are dead, but I am afraid they are not alive.

Our mother desires her love and hopes to hear from you.

Your affectionate sister,
E.C.

My Dear Charlotte,

You will be pleased to learn that our fossiling party was most successful. True, Miss Blair, the governess, being a timid soul, was in a state of agitation whenever the boys scrambled too far up the rocks or seemed likely to plunge into rock pools in pursuit of the finest specimens. She was also concerned when I gave them the hammers, presumably imagining that they were to use them upon each other rather than upon the stones. However, I managed to persuade her that there was no danger by scrambling among the rocks myself, though I fear she was shocked at what she obviously considered unsuitable behaviour on my part.

It was charming, though, to see the boys' pleasure, and they were forever expressing their delight in simple ammonites and demanding of me information as to their formation etc. I have promised to unearth Frank's 'museum' of such things for their greater edification, though where it may now be found I do not know. I beg you will try to bring it to mind for I would be loth to disappoint them. When I brought them back to Monkton our mother was delighted with them and later told me that George put her greatly in mind of William at that age. She insisted on their turning out their pockets to exhibit their treasures—dismissing Miss Blair's cries of horror at the sand scattered on the carpet in the process—which were greatly admired.

While I was occupied in offering them cakes and sweetmeats, you will not be surprised to hear that our mother was quizzing Miss Blair who, it seems, is the daughter of a clergyman in Kent who, owing to a superfluity of sisters, is obliged to take up governessing. She is of a timid disposition and greatly in awe of Sir Edward, who, however, treats her with perfect civility. She is also, poor soul, very apprehensive about finding a new position when the boys go to school next year, and our mother has requested us both to cast about among our acquaintance to see if any of them might require her services. It seems that Miss Blair was appointed by Sir Edward's wife when he was abroad, a few years before she died. Miss Blair was full of praise and admiration for her late mistress who was the only daughter of a close friend of Sir Edward's father, and I gather that the match was made without much consultation of the parties on either side. However, since the bride had considerable beauty and an amiable disposition, I do not think Sir Edward raised many objections to the match. Sadly it transpired that she was also delicate and she died of an inflammation of the lungs two years ago. Do you not agree that our mother is a nonpareil at discovering people's histories!

After making a hearty meal the boys went away with many thanks and requests for another expedition. It would be an excellent thing to take them to Charmouth where even finer specimens are to be found, though I am not certain that our father would consider favourably my use of the carriage for such a venture.

Yesterday I went to Layton's and bought what I intended to buy, but not in much perfection. There was scarcely any knotting silk; but Layton says he will be going to Exeter next week and will lay in a stock. I gave 2s3d. a yard for my flannel, and I fancy it is not very good, but it is so disgraceful and contemptible an article in itself that its not being comparatively good or bad is of little importance.

I was considering what you had to say about the kitchen at Holcombe Park and how it seems to have been so full of people coming and going that it would, in the general confusion, not be impossible to have introduced some fatal substance into Mrs Churchill's food or posset. Perhaps Sarah may remember if there were any dishes that only Mrs Woodstock partook of or if anyone was there later in the evening when the posset may have been left unguarded. Not that it is by any means certain that Mrs Woodstock was poisoned; her death, as you have suggested may have been caused by some other means.

It is, as you say, fortunate that Mary is so interested in the story as to have forgotten her own troubles for the moment and I will do my best to keep you provided with any tid-bit of information that may excite her curiosity and thereby promote her better temper to the benefit of you all.

Yours affectionately,
E.C.

My Dear Charlotte,

As you have by this time received my last letter, it is fit that I should begin another, though I have but a slender budget of news for you. The only event of any note was the return of Mr James Russell. I saw him yesterday morning on the Parade. Since I could see no difference to the style of his hair when he raised his hat (an elegant grey beaver) in salutation, I conclude that Sir Edward's conjecture was without foundation. It would seem that he had gone up to London to settle some matters of business and to fetch his valet.

"Since," he said, "I am likely to be making a longer stay in this delightful town than I had anticipated it would be quite impossible for me to do without Corbett any longer."

"Then you are settled here in Lyme, sir, for the immediate future?"

"I do feel my place is by my uncle's side, especially since this tiresome business about my aunt's death has greatly upset him. I had hoped that when Sir Matthew returned to London we had heard the last of the matter, but it seems that Sir Edward Hampton has taken it upon himself to pursue it and his visits to Holcombe have greatly distressed my uncle."

"I believe, sir, that he is simply doing his duty as a magistrate, having been called upon to act by Sir Matthew, and I am sure he feels the business to be as tiresome as you do."

"Well, yes, of course," he said hastily, "I understand that he must act. Indeed my cousin spoke very highly of him and is anxious that we should give him all assistance so that a speedy resolution can be achieved. Meanwhile it is a great pleasure to be back once again with all my friends in Lyme."

It will be interesting to see *which* of his friends he seeks out and if he still maintains his distance from Miss West and what, indeed, his intentions are towards her.

"I fear we will miss your company next week at the Assembly Rooms," I said.

"As to that, I may look in—not to dance, of course, but simply to renew my acquaintance with those friends that I spoke of."

"I am sure they will be very glad to see you. Will Mr Rivers be with you? I believe he is also staying on in Lyme."

"Yes indeed. Frederick has some matters still to conclude with my uncle and he too will not wish to leave before this wretched business of my aunt's death is settled. And I shall hope to encourage him to join me at the Assembly where we will both, I know, hope to have the pleasure of *your* company." So I am determined to watch Mr Russell and Miss West very carefully so that I may have some more interesting news to send to you next week.

As to our Mystery, tell Mary that Lucy has it from Sarah that the Wests' maid Deborah was indeed in the kitchen at Holcombe on the evening of Mrs Woodstock's death. It seems that she has struck up a friendship with the Woodstock's cook and is there quite often. I am sure that you and Mary between you should be able to make something quite remarkable of that!

I am extremely glad that you like the poplin. I thought it would have our mother's approbation, but was not so confident of yours. Remember it is a present. Do not refuse me.

Your affectionate sister,

E.C.

My Dear Charlotte,

You will wish me, I am sure, to furnish you and Mary with an account of the Assembly last evening. As for dancing it was very poor, only fifteen couple and but forty people in the room, few families indeed from our side of the county and not many more from the other. It was felt to be unfortunate that two of the more personable men (by which I mean Mr Russell and Mr Rivers) were not dancing, but the reason that they were not doing so—the death of their near relative—was very fine for conversation.

As I mentioned in my last letter, I was eager to see in what manner Mr Russell and Miss West conducted themselves. Miss West—in blue crape with ribbon trimmings—and her mother arrived first. I saw Mrs West casting glances round the room as if searching for someone, and, when Mr Russell arrived with his cousin, she said something to her daughter (which alas I could not hear) that caused her to look annoyed, but another word from her mother appeared to subdue her.

Upon Captain Tilson asking her to dance she accepted, slightly reluctantly though her mother nodded approval. I observed, however, that, in the course of the dance, Miss West glanced quite often towards that part of the room where Mr Russell was in conversation with Mrs Holder. Since he was not dancing he had every excuse for not approaching Miss West—he did bow as he passed them on the way to speak to Mr Holder, but that was all. Mr Rivers, on the other hand, was most attentive. I think I told you that he was previously much struck with Miss West and, certainly, appeared determined to pursue the acquaintance. To my surprise Mrs West seemed positively to encourage the attention. Perhaps she hopes to make Mr Russell so jealous as to bring him to the point. Whatever her reason I cannot but be sorry for Mr Rivers since there is no likelihood of Mrs West's taking the lesser prize for her daughter.

I could not follow Mr Rivers' progress since young Tom Chamberlyne, at home from Oxford, asked me to dance and, in all conscience, I couldn't bring myself to hurt his feelings by refusing him, though it meant taking my eye off the drama.

When I had returned to my place Mrs West had departed into the card room and Miss West was dancing with one of the sons of Mr and Mrs Cooke who, you may remember, have an estate near Axminster.

In spite of his declared wish to renew his acquaintance with his friends at Lyme, Mr Russell did not stay long—we had a brief conversation about very little—and went away quite soon, taking his cousin with him. I noticed, as they left, that Mr Rivers looked wistfully at Miss West, dancing with one of Captain Tilson's brother officers, whose name I do not know, as if he would like to have stayed. However, he dutifully followed his cousin home.

Poor Miss Craven and her mama must have been sadly disappointed. Without Mrs Woodstock's eye upon him, Mr Russell exchanged the merest civilities with them and made his escape as soon as he decently could. But Miss Craven may still find a husband. She is, for the most part, silent and not ill-looking if one can overlook her freckles, and I am sure that may easily be done by contemplation of her fortune, so I shall not feel sorry for her.

So it would appear that Mr Russell has not yet broached the subject of his engagement (if such it be) to his uncle. I suppose he feels it is too soon after his aunt's death and he may not yet be sure of his inheritance. Also the circumstances of the death being what they are, he would not wish it to be known that there was any reason he wished his aunt ill. There, I have given you a motive! though I am sure we are already agreed that Mr Russell is the most likely person to have benefited from his aunt's death.

You must tell Robert that our father gives 25s. apiece to Seward for his last lot of sheep, and in return for this news, our father wishes to receive news of Robert's pigs. He was interested to learn that farmer Claringbould had died and that Robert means to get some of his farm. Please let him know how this plan progresses.

I forgot to say that the evening was cool enough for me to wear my new muslin shawl which gave me great satisfaction though no-one remarked upon it.

Your affectionate sister,
E.C.

My Dear Charlotte,

Your letter has brought its usual measure of satisfaction and amusement. Your offer of cravats is very kind, and happens to be particularly adapted to my wants, but it was an odd thing to occur to you.

Yesterday brought a visit from Sir Edward to our father who invited him to remain to dine with us. I am sure our mother was relieved that we had planned a respectable saddle of mutton for today, which Cook roasted to perfection. Had he come yesterday he would have had to suffer one of my experiments, viz: ox cheek with dumplings—excellent fare to be sure but not to be offered to Sir Edward Hampton of Marshwood Abbey. Our mother took the opportunity of demanding of Sir Edward what progress he had made in his investigation and was anxious to be assured that Dr King could in no wise be held in any way responsible for what might or might not have happened.

"I do believe," he said, "that Dr King did all that might be expected of him. Since I believe Mrs Woodstock had always complained of ill health there can hardly have been a suspicion that her death was anything but natural."

"I imagine," our father said "that Dr King, above all others, was aware that Mrs Woodstock's illnesses were usually a means of getting her own way and did not indicate any disease or a less than robust constitution."

Sir Edward was silent for a moment and then he said with a sigh "Indeed, sir, this brings home what a disadvantage it is to me to be obliged to pursue this matter having but recently come into the county. I have no knowledge of the people concerned or what might be the reason for this crime—if, indeed, crime there be."

Our mother, divided between a desire to protect Dr King from any imputation of negligence in not remarking upon the cause of Mrs Woodstock's death and the pleasure of having a real mystery upon our very doorstep, ventured to remark that there may well have been several persons who might have benefited from her death.

Sir Edward said "That may be true. Indeed, it must be unusual to find any death about which this might not be said."

Our mother, who, as you know, takes no account of satirical remarks, continued, "Well, have you considered James Russell? He has a great deal to gain by his aunt's death."

"Indeed? I was not aware that he was her heir."

"Mrs Woodstock made him an allowance that let him live in London in great style, but she kept him on a very tight rein—he was always at her beck and call. But now she is gone he can bring his uncle round to do whatever he pleases."

Our father, displeased at the turn the conversation had taken, interrupted to ask Sir Edward about the prospects for the coming season's shooting and no more was said about it. However, I saw that Sir Edward appeared to take note of what our mother had said and will presumably consider it.

Later when the tray came in and our mother was pouring the tea and when our father had gone to find some documents he wanted our guest to see, Sir Edward thanked me for the treat I had given his boys.

"It was my pleasure, sir. It gave me the excuse to indulge in a pastime that has long been a favourite in this family."

"George tells me that there are even finer specimens at Charmouth."

"Certainly there are—the cliffs there are more extensive than at Lyme and so there is a greater variety."

"You are well informed, Miss Cowper," he said.

"As I said, sir, it has long been a family pastime."

"Then perhaps it might be agreeable to you to accompany my sons there on another expedition?"

"I would be very happy to do so, sir, but I fear we must wait a while for the opportunity. It is still a busy time of the year and my father requires the horses for the farm."

"I would not dream of putting your father to that inconvenience and would of course send my carriage to convey you if you will let me know which day will suit you."

"That would be most kind of you, sir."

"On the contrary, the kindness is all on your side Miss Cowper."

"I can assure you that I will take as much pleasure as the boys may in such an expedition."

Our mother, who had caught my reference to the boys, broke in with praise of them, commenting on their liveliness and intelligence. "George puts me in mind of William at that age," she said, "and John has much of Frank's enquiring mind, wanting to know the why and wherefore of everything."

"I trust, ma'am that they were not troublesome to you."

"Oh no, it is delightful to see high spirits in boys of their age—it was a great pleasure to see them."

"I fear they have now outgrown their governess and I am glad that they will be soon gone to school. Meanwhile I am most grateful to Miss Cowper for her interest in them and for the time she has given to their entertainment."

"Oh Elinor always liked scrambling about among the rocks with her brothers; Charlotte did not care for it."

And, indeed, dear Charlotte I remember many lectures you gave me about my unladylike behaviour, when I walked back through the town with my petticoats muddy and bedraggled from searching for fossils when the tide had just gone out, which Frank always said was a splendid time to find them.

Our father coming back into the room, the conversation turned to a certain boundary dispute he was concerned about for one of his tenants. However, before he left, Sir Edward arranged to send his carriage next Tuesday if the weather should be fine.

Mrs Holder's niece, Miss Porter, is recently come into the neighbourhood but is not much admired; the good-natured world, as usual, extolled her beauty so highly, that all of Lyme have had the pleasure of being disappointed

I called yesterday on old Betty, who inquired particularly after you, and said she seemed to miss you very much because you used to call on her very often. This was an oblique reproach to me, which I am sorry to have merited, and from which I will profit.

I am quite angry with myself for not writing closer; why is my alphabet so much more sprawly than yours?

Yours affectionately,
E.C.

My Dear Charlotte,

We were glad to hear that Mary's new nurse is come but sorry to hear that Mary thinks she has no particular charm either of person or manner; but as all the neighbourhood pronounces her to be the best nurse that ever was and since Mary is finding the baby fretful and tiring, I expect her attachment to increase.

Sir Edward's carriage duly arrived, but with Sir Edward in it. I had expected only the boys and their governess and was greatly surprised by this addition to the party.

"I trust you will not object," he said observing this, "to another member of the expedition, but George was anxious that I should see for myself the wonders of the shore that you have revealed to them. He did even offer to let me have the use of the small hammer which you were so kind as to lend him."

"You are most welcome, sir," I said. Indeed I could hardly say otherwise since he had provided the carriage.

Our journey to Charmouth was enlivened by eager questions from the boys as to the finds my brothers had made and where the finest specimens were to be found. Miss Blair occasionally remonstrated with them when their voices rose too loud, but, poor soul, she was constrained by the unaccustomed presence of her employer, and her faint protests were, in the main, ignored.

On our arrival at Charmouth we left the carriage and made our way down that path, which you will remember leads down to the shore. It was a fine day, though not warm, and I was glad that I was wearing my kerseymere spenser. The boys ran on ahead with Miss Blair while we followed more sedately behind. However, once we reached the shore I was much in demand for knowing which rocks they should strike and, when they had done so, what were the names of the treasures thus revealed.

After a while, Sir Edward, who had joined his sons among the rocks and had been fossiling with them with apparent enjoyment, rejoined me where I was in conversation with Miss Blair. "I think we may leave them to themselves for a while," he said. "I am sure, Miss Cowper, you deserve a rest from their importunities. They will come to no harm if Miss Blair will keep an eye on them." Miss Blair moved nearer her charges and Sir Edward continued,

"This seems a convenient and tolerably comfortable boulder if you would be seated. I would be grateful for your advice on a certain subject."

As you can imagine, My Dear Charlotte, I was greatly surprised. I had assumed from his general attitude that Sir Edward has no great opinion of the female sex and could not imagine on what subject he would welcome my advice.

"Indeed, sir, my mother and sister will assure you that I am always delighted to give my advice upon any subject, whether I am asked for it or no."

He gave the half smile which seems to be the furthest he is prepared to go in this respect, and said, "It concerns the fact that, as a new-comer, I have no knowledge of the people who may or may not have to do with the death of Mrs Woodstock. Therefore, I wondered if I might prevail upon the members of your family to aid me. Your father has most kindly been of invaluable assistance to me in many ways since I came into the neighbourhood and I feel he is the one person I can turn to for help in this matter. I am aware that he is naturally most reluctant to seem to be gossiping about his neighbours, but do you think he might be persuaded that it is in the interest of a legal investigation to make me acquainted with the histories and characters of persons who may be concerned?"

"You wish help from all the members of his family, sir?"

"Your mother, too. I am sure she is on terms with everyone involved and would, I think, be willing to pass on any opinions she might have."

"I am sure my mother would be delighted to help you, and, if it is put to him that it is his duty to support the law in this way, I do not believe that my father would have any objection to passing on to you his thoughts on anything arising in the course of your investigations."

"And you, Miss Cowper?"

"You wish for *my* opinions, sir?"

"Most certainly I do. It appears to me that you have a very keen eye for the flaws and foibles of your fellow creatures."

"That sounds a most disagreeable quality!"

"No, for I believe it springs from a wish to perceive the true nature of a person. And that, you must agree, would be invaluable."

As you will imagine, this very odd remark took me quite by surprise so that I did not immediately reply.

"Well, Miss Cowper," he asked "will you help me?"

And, of course, the temptation to be involved in our Mystery was not to be resisted, so what could I do but agree?

Our father requires you to tell Robert that one of his Leicestershire sheep, sold to the butcher last week, weighed 27 lb. and 1/4 per quarter. I do not know precisely what this means, but no doubt Robert will understand.

I am sure you will be interested to know how our father responds to Sir Edward's proposal—I will do my duty and keep you fully informed.

I do not remember if I told you that Mrs Heathcote wrote to tell us that Miss Blackford is married, but I have never seen it in the papers, and one may as well be single if the wedding is not in print.

Your affectionate sister,
E.C.

My Dear Charlotte,

Your letter yesterday gave me some amusement, Mary's comments being so far wide of the mark. While it is true that Sir Edward is in the comfortable possession of *two* estates and must, I suppose, be considered eligible, do assure her that he is not so regarded by me! A widower! and with two grown boys! Putting aside the fact that he is nearer my father's age than mine, you must have noted that I find his manner and address on the whole stiff and lacking in ease. It is true that he unbends when he is with his children—a point in his favour certainly, but, as you know, I have always held that dullness in a man, whatever his wealth, makes him quite ineligible. It may be that our future conversations about the Woodstock mystery will lend *some* animation to our discourse, but even Mary could not expect an alliance to prosper with so little in common.

I beg you will prevent Mary from putting such ideas into our mother's head! Sir Edward already stands high in her esteem by his favourable comments on Dr King, and I have no doubt but that she will be delighted to give him the benefit of her opinion of all our acquaintance if our father does not intervene.

You will be interested to learn that Mr Powlett gave a dance on Thursday, to the great disturbance of his neighbours, who, you know, take a most lively interest in the state of his finances, and live in the hope of his soon being ruined.

I met Miss West yesterday coming out of Layton's. She greeted me with the familiarity of an old friend and suggested we walk together along the Parade. "Since it is such a fine day and I am sure that exercise and sea air will benefit us both." A sentiment I would agree with, but naturally resented as coming from one whose opinions on any matter I am not inclined to receive.

"I do not believe I have seen you, Miss West, since the Assembly," I said.

"Indeed, I was not certain of being able to attend since I had been unwell almost up to the very day."

"How fortunate that you had recovered in time to attend."

"Oh mama made me her tincture of bark—very much superior to Huxham's—and I recovered very rapidly."

"Mrs West is skilled in tinctures and draughts?"

"Oh she was noted for her knowledge of herbs and remedies by all in Tonbridge."

"How very fortunate that you had such excellent remedies to hand so that you were able to attend the Assembly, though it was, I fear, very thin of company."

"I was most surprised. It was not very entertaining. At Tonbridge we rarely had fewer than two and thirty couple."

"Indeed I do not wonder you found it dull, though I am sure *you* did not lack for partners even though both Mr Russell and Mr Rivers were not dancing."

"No, they could hardly do so in the circumstances." She was silent for a while and then she said, "Miss Cowper, the information I gave you, regarding Mr Russell and myself...."

"Yes?"

"You may have thought it odd that Mr Russell has made no announcement."

"About your engagement? No, indeed, it would have been most unsuitable to have made such an announcement at such a time."

"That is what mama tells me and that I must learn to be patient for things will come out right in the end."

"I am sure, Miss West, that your mother has the matter very much in hand."

"Oh, do you think so?"

"I am sure of it." And I *am* convinced that Mrs West will do everything in her power to make sure that her scheme succeeds.

"You have told no-one of our engagement?" she enquired anxiously. I assured her that her secret is safe, since I am persuaded that *you* will not betray it. "Mama says it is very important that dear James should seek an appropriate time to tell his uncle of our plans, especially, she says, since the case is complicated by the circumstances of Mrs Woodstock's death."

"Of course."

"I cannot imagine why that horrid Sir Matthew should make such a fuss about it, bringing in Sir Edward to cause all this commotion. Do you know Sir Edward, Miss Cowper? What manner of man is he?"

"I believe he is a sensible man who will do his duty as a magistrate."

She sighed. "That is what mama says and it is so tiresome that this stupid business should put off our announcement. James has not called upon us once since it started and he barely spoke to me at the Assembly."

Miss West, I must tell you, was wearing a most unusual bonnet decorated with fruit—cherries and Orleans plums—which you may think presented an odd appearance, but, infact, was quite charming, though, of course it is more natural to have flowers growing out of the head than fruit!

You are very kind in planning presents for me to make, and our mother has shown me exactly the same attention; but as I do not choose to have generosity dictated to me, I shall not resolve on giving my little cabinet to Anne till the first thought has been my own.

I have been much exercised in my mind as to whether I should tell Sir Edward about James Russell's secret engagement as it was, after all, told to me in confidence. Since you, My Dear Charlotte, have always been the keeper of my conscience, I appeal to you for guidance in this matter. My own inclination is to remain silent until circumstances force my hand, though I do admit that this is mere procrastination, ever a fault of mine as you will be the first to point out.

You ask about the black butter. The first pot was opened and proved not at all what it ought to be; it was neither solid nor entirely sweet, and on seeing it Lucy remembered that you had said you did not think it had been boiled enough. Such being the event of the first pot, we did not save the second, and therefore ate it in unpretending privacy; and part of it was very good.

Our mother joins with me in sending love to Mary and the dear children

Yours affectionately,
E.C.

My Dear Charlotte,

I was not surprised at your answer to my problem, having anticipated the one even before I put the other. You are quite in the right, of course, to say that I must tell Sir Edward of Mr Russell's secret engagement, since he needs to be in full possession of the facts so that he may make a proper judgement. So much for right and reason. I, however, in my own unreasonable way am still reluctant to do so and will leave it awhile to see what else may happen. So the scrupulously right and proper thing may be laid to one side to accommodate another sort of scruple entirely! All of which would make a very pretty sermon for Mr Wilmot if I were able to put it to him.

We have seen nothing of Sir Edward so far, but our father did speak to our mother and to me about the matter, saying that indeed it was our duty to give Sir Edward what information was necessary for the advancement of the enquiry but he knew that we would never condescend to mere gossip. Our mother and I readily gave our consent, though we were both aware that our father's idea of gossip is in many respects quite different from our own.

Our mother, incidentally, has been lately adding to her possession in plate—a whole tablespoon and a whole dessert spoon, and six whole teaspoons—which makes our sideboard border on the magnificent.

I wish I could help you with your needlework—Mary must be grateful to have so much done—since I have two hands and a new thimble that lead a very easy life.

Mrs Holden called upon us yesterday with news of poor Mr Woodstock who has been very low since the death of his wife. One would have thought he might have regarded it as a happy release from the tyranny she exercised over him but it appears that he is lost without someone to tell him what to do and what to think. The wild beast released from its cage after many years is not more reluctant to venture forth than he is. It may be that when he has had a sufficient taste of freedom and is grown more accustomed to the state, he may yet regain his spirits. Meanwhile he has become more weak and uncertain than ever and his condition is not helped by the questioning of his household (necessary I now admit) about his wife's death, all of which brings on nervous spasms that require the attendance of Dr King.

Mrs Holder says that Mr James Russell has been no support, being either away or, when he is in Lyme, unheeding of his uncle's distress and absorbed in his own affairs. If it were not for Mr Rivers' kindness and sympathy, she says, poor Mr Woodstock would be in a sorry state.

Our mother is now determined that we should call upon him and thus find out for herself how matters stand, so I should be able to furnish you with first hand news of the household at Holcombe Park. I am surprised that Mr Russell has not sought to ingratiate himself with his uncle to prepare him for the news of his engagement, but perhaps he, too, is a procrastinator, waiting for the right moment, which may never come.

I am *not* surprised, however, to learn that Mr Rivers is doing all that is proper to comfort his cousin. He seems to me to be an excellent sort of man, reliable and just the sort of person one would call upon, and I am sure Mr Woodstock cannot but be grateful to have him here at hand and not in the far Barbados. I do hope that Mr Rivers has not set his mind on Miss West for, not only do I think his hopes would be dashed by Miss West's mama, but I would be sad to see a sensible man entrapped by mere beauty, something one sees only too often, as we have had cause to remark.

Our mother wants to know if Robert has ever made the henhouse which they planned together. I am glad to hear that Robert's income is a good one—as glad as I can be at anybody's being rich except you and me—and I am thoroughly rejoiced to hear of his and Mary's present to you.

Yours affectionately,
E.C.

My Dear Charlotte,

Though you will scarcely have received my last letter, I take up my pen again to tell you of our visit to Holcombe Park. Mr Woodstock greeted us most warmly, being glad, I think, to have his old friends about him. Mr James Russell was not to be seen, being gone to Exeter it is said to conduct some business for his uncle but, mostly probably, to escape the dismal atmosphere at home.

You will be amused to learn that Mr Woodstock has taken on some of the qualities of his late wife and is now forever complaining of some indisposition or other—he who scarcely dared to have a headache is now enjoying a variety of illnesses which require the almost constant attention of Dr King. We were invited to take luncheon with him and although the refreshments provided were of the usual lavishness and excellence, all Mr Woodstock would take was a bowl of gruel. "For I find," he said, "that, at this hour, anything else produces a colicky condition. Dr King thinks that I may benefit from taking the waters, so that when all this sorry business is settled I may go to Bath."

So much for *Mrs* Woodstock's preference for Cheltenham! But I am glad for Mr Woodstock, that he has found an occupation for himself that will (quite easily) recompense him for his loss.

Mr Rivers was in attendance and was most kind and attentive to his cousin. Our mother asked him how long he would remain in England.

"Well, as to that," he said, "I do not know. I am glad to be of use to my cousin and fortunately I have a good manager in Barbados who is perfectly able to look after the Estate. Of course, I miss my son but he is greatly attached to his grandparents and lives with them. But for the present my duty lies here."

Mr Woodstock nodded approvingly at this and said, "Frederick is a capital fellow and I don't know how I would manage without him!" I wondered how Mr James Russell felt about this dependence and if he was concerned that Mr Rivers was gaining too much influence over his relative. But if he cannot be bothered to take trouble with his uncle he will only have himself to blame if he finds his inheritance given to another. I can only suppose he feels himself so secure he need not bother with anything so tiresome as attending upon an old man. Which merely confirms what we have always thought: that Mr James Russell is a very foolish young man indeed. However, by no means do I accuse Mr Rivers of being devious in this matter. I find him a person of excellent character with a sympathetic nature and believe that he is truly sorry for his cousin and wishes to do all in his power to assist him.

When we left our mother was very scornful of Mr Woodstock. "To be forever coddling himself and having poor Dr King running back and forth whenever he fancies himself ill! I have no patience with him and I think Mr Rivers is a remarkably amiable young man to put up with him. I was asking him about Chapman—after all she was Mrs Woodstock's personal maid and now her mistress is no more I was surprised to learn that she is still there. However, it seems that although Chapman is anxious to go and live with her sister in Seaton—and Mr Woodstock is to give her a handsome annuity—she has been required to remain until this investigation is finished, which is quite ridiculous and when I see Sir Edward I will certainly tell him so!"

I forgot to tell you in my last letter that you need not endeavour to match our mother's morning calico; she does not mean to make it up any more.

Yesterday we had a letter from Nanny Hilliard, the object of which is that she would be very much obliged to us if we could get Hannah a place. I am sorry that we cannot assist her; if you can think of anywhere—or if Mary can—let me know, as I shall not answer the letter immediately.

Your affectionate sister,
E.C.

My Dear Charlotte,

Sir Edward called today and, our father being out at the farm, our mother seized the opportunity of speaking her mind on the subject of our neighbours with no restraining presence! "Far be it from me to speak ill of the dead, Sir Edward, but it seems to me that many people will lead easier lives now that Mrs Woodstock is no more. Not, of course, that she was not a worthy woman in many ways, a pillar of society, you might say, with very high standards and moral principles. But not an easy woman to live with, if you understand me. How poor Mr Woodstock survived, harried and bullied all his days I shall never know."

"You don't imagine that Mr Woodstock had anything to do with her death?" Sir Edward enquired.

"Good gracious no, whatever gave you that idea! No, poor man, he couldn't say boo to a goose, let alone his wife. But she did make life most difficult for poor Mr Russell, her nephew. His father died—he was in the army, serving somewhere abroad, I can't remember where—and his mother, although she was of a good family, had no fortune of her own so that they were really quite poor and Mr Russell was dependent on his aunt for the elegancies of life—well you know, Sir Edward how young men have no sense of money—though we have been most fortunate in our two sons who are *most* sensible about such things, beside the fact that Mr Cowper has always brought them up to live within their means. No, Mr Russell was what I might call an *expensive* young man and he knew he had to dance to her tune if she was going to supply him with horses, carriages and I know not what. Always down here whenever she lifted her little finger or pretended to be at death's door. Well, she played that trick one time too many and now she really is dead."

"Do you mean you think that Mr Russell may have in some way caused her death?" Sir Edward said.

"Goodness me, what an idea! Oh no, Mr Russell is a very nice, well-spoken young man, always most polite and attentive. They say that he might offer for Miss Craven—she is something of an heiress you know but now that his Aunt has died he may not be obliged to do so..."

Here Lucy came in to require our mother's presence in the kitchen on some domestic matter and she was obliged to leave us alone.

"And what is your view of Mr Russell?" Sir Edward asked. "Do you share your mother's opinion?"

"I think Mr Russell is a fashionable young man who looked to his aunt to keep him handsomely fitted out. I believe she was fond of him, after her fashion, and was quite happy to indulge him provided he showed her attention."

"She had a fortune of her own?"

"Since they had no children of their own, I believe Mr Woodstock looked upon him as his heir and, being easily swayed, will no doubt continue to indulge Mr Russell as his wife did, and without the demands she made upon him."

"So, other than the tiresome business of having to wait upon his aunt's pleasure, Mr Russell had no reason to wish her dead?"

I must admit, My Dear Charlotte, that I was within a moment of telling him of Miss West, but that scruple I mentioned to you before held me back. I know you will not approve of it, though you will credit me, I hope, with not giving a downright lie, but remaining silent.

"I believe," he continued, "that he and Mr Woodstock were the only people dining with Mrs Woodstock that evening. Mr Rivers was not there?"

"No, he dined with us that evening."

"You know Mr Rivers well?"

"He has but lately come into the neighbourhood, having been in Barbados for many years, so he is a new acquaintance—though a very pleasant one."

"Indeed? And what is your opinion of him?"

"It is, I believe, the general opinion. That he is a very amiable man, pleasant company and with great good sense."

"You approve of good sense then, Miss Cowper?"

"Does not every rational person?"

Our mother just then coming back into the room, she resumed the conversation. "Were you talking of Mr Rivers? Now he is a charming man! Mrs Holder was telling me that at one of the Assemblies, although he would certainly have wished to be dancing he made no objection to making up a four at whist when Mrs Chamberlyne asked him. And his manner is always so agreeable, nothing is too much trouble for him. Why, when Mrs Brompton was laid up with a cold he went all the way to Exeter to procure some special wool she needed to complete a carpet she was making. And when he dined with us he was able to converse easily with Mr Mildmay, who is quite deaf and needs a good deal of trouble to make him hear—a great problem on such occasions, and I have often said to Mr Cowper that only the fact that he is one of our oldest friends persuades me to invite him! No, Mr Rivers is a splendid addition to our society and I for one will be very sorry to see him go back to Barbados."

"I see you all have golden opinions of him, ma'am."

"Indeed I do and I cannot imagine what Mr Woodstock would have done without him these last weeks. Especially now that he—Mr Woodstock, that is—has taken to invalidish ways. He was talking the other day of oppressions in his head. Well I told him that such an attack is quite usual at his age. Last year I had for some time the sensation of a peck loaf resting on my head, and they talked of cupping me, but Dr King gave me a dose or two of calomel and I've never heard of it since!"

I think it was with some relief that Sir Edward greeted our father who had just returned from the farm and they went off into the Library where I have no doubt they had an enjoyable conversation about the harvest and the prospects for the shooting season.

Our mother was delighted with Sir Edward, pronouncing him a man of sense whose opinions she heartily agreed with.

How is your blue gown? Mine is all in pieces. I think there must have been something wrong in the dye, for in places it divided with a touch. There was four shillings thrown away, to be added to my subjects of never-failing regret.

Today's unpromising aspect makes it absolutely necessary for me to observe how peculiarly fortunate you have been with your weather. We will be obliged to start fires soon.

Yours affectionately,
E.C.

My Dear Charlotte,

You will like to know that we had a very pleasant party yesterday. Only six guests—the Chamberlynes, Maria Brompton, Mr Rivers, Mr Russell and Sir Edward. Mr Woodstock was invited but declared that he dare not face the chill winds of autumn, a remark which our mother was inclined to scorn until he added that Dr King had expressly forbidden him to do so.

The mutton was well cooked, since I had made several visits to the kitchen to be sure that Cook did not persist in serving it up in the under-done state she prefers, and the fowl was likewise well received. Remarking upon the excellence of the syllabub, Mrs Chamberlyne exclaimed that it was something Mrs Woodstock had particularly liked and that it was always prepared for every dinner at Holcombe Park on the chance that she might fancy it. At this I noticed that Sir Edward was regarding Mr Russell and Mr Rivers most intently and I wondered if he believed something fatal might have been introduced into the dish that might have caused Mrs Woodstock's death. However, as far as I could judge, neither young man reacted in any way oddly so that Sir Edward's conjecture—whatever it might have been—was abandoned.

The introduction of Mrs Woodstock's name allowed other guests to comment upon the events of the past weeks though the presence of two of her relations naturally confined the comments to the favourable rather than the candid.

"Such a loss to our small society," Mrs Chamberlyne said.

"Greatly missed," Maria Brompton contributed, and turning to Sir Edward, she asked him what progress was being made in discovering the facts of her death.

Sir Edward, who is undoubtedly heartily sick of such questions, answered her with politeness, though with a discouraging brevity.

Our father, who had observed Sir Edward's irritation, turned the subject to the proposed alterations to the quay and the conversation became less general. Mr Rivers, who was sitting on my left, enquired after the health of one of the children of Bates at the farm, who has been sick of a fever and whom Mr

Rivers has visited on several occasions. I observed that it was most kind of him to take an interest in poor Jem and he said, "I heard of the child's condition and, having certain medicines I have found efficacious in treating people on the estate in Barbados, I hoped I might be of some assistance."

"Indeed," I said "he is greatly improved and his parents are truly grateful to you for the trouble you have taken. You have a knowledge of medicines?"

"Hardly that, but I have been accustomed to do what I can if there is illness. We have a doctor but he lives some distance away so it is often necessary to give some sort of assistance until he arrives, so I have tried to make a study of medicines that might be useful. When Mr Wilmot told me of the child I thought I might be of help and the draught I gave him – something I have made up myself – did reduce the fever."

"It was, indeed, good of you to do so and I am sure Mr Wilmot was also grateful. The Bates do not live in his parish, which is Charton, but the living of this parish of Westover, which adjoins Charton, has recently fallen vacant so there is no clergyman present in Westover. The living is in Mr Woodstock's gift and we were hoping that he might give it to Mr Wilmot, who is such a worthy man."

"That would excellent. I will certainly do all I can to persuade my cousin to agree to such a plan."

So it may be that Mr Wilmot will get the preferment he deserves. Indeed, it may be possible for him to combine the two livings, that of Westover is, I believe, worth 150*l* a year and, together with the wretched 50*l* at Charton, it would provide a reasonable income. Indeed he might even marry on it, should he find a wife of similarly frugal inclinations as himself.

Certainly it was kind of Mr Rivers to offer his support and we must hope that he succeeds in persuading Mr Woodstock.

I thought Mr Russell was not in the best of spirits, which is surprising considering that he is now free of his tyrant aunt and has every prospect of a richer and more agreeable life. It may be, of course that he is being urged by Mrs West to make public his engagement, but I do not believe she would push him too hard at this moment for fear of losing him altogether. Certainly, although he appeared to be listening to Maria

Brompton's account of the latest movements of the militia and the effect they may have on our Assemblies, it was obvious to me that his mind was elsewhere.

After the tea tray was brought in Sir Edward came to speak to me.

"Mr Rivers seems to be a most agreeable man," he said "full of conversation and with an easy manner. I can quite see why he is universally popular."

"Indeed," I said "and he has been most kind to the son of my father's tenant. The poor child has been suffering from a fever and Mr Rivers, hearing of it, immediately went to take him medicines that greatly relieved the symptoms."

"I did not know that Mr Rivers was a medical man."

"He is not, but he is accustomed to help care for the people on Mr Woodstock's estate in Barbados in times of sickness. He gave poor Jem a draught he had made up himself."

"Did he indeed? A draught that he made up himself?"

"Yes. It greatly reduced the fever."

"So Mr Rivers is expert in making medicines, is he?"

I looked at him in amazement. "Oh come now, Sir Edward, surely you are not suggesting that Mr Rivers had anything to do with Mrs Woodstock's death. He is the kindest of men—why he has just now been telling me that he is to try to persuade his cousin to give the living of Westover to Mr Wilmot, such a deserving man who badly needs the preferment."

"Mr Rivers is a paragon indeed."

"But what possible reason could he have for wishing Mrs Woodstock's death? To be sure she bullied and abused him, but then, she did so to everyone around her."

"I am sure you are right, Miss Cowper and I apologise for having thought the worst of such a universal favourite."

Our mother, having completed her duties at the tea tray, called Sir Edward over to her to enquire about the welfare of his two sons.

"Such delightful boys, Sir Edward and it was a pleasure to have children about the house again."

"Indeed, ma'am, they greatly enjoyed their visit and George, in particular, continues to speak of the splendid specimens *your* sons have collected."

"They must come again and Elinor will get out some of the things from Frank's *Exhibition,* for so he called it. Elinor, you will not mind looking out all those strange objects that Frank had to show them to Sir Edward's boys?"

"I hesitate to trouble Miss Cowper," he said "when she has already been so kind."

"Not at all," I said "I will be happy to do so."

So now, dear Charlotte, I am obliged to search the school-room for all Frank's treasures, a task which will be as dusty as it is tiresome. Still, it will give our mother pleasure to have the house full of young voices. I do not believe she was ever happier than when we were all young, a singular preference, though I believe that is the way with mothers everywhere!

We have just had two hampers of apples from Kintbury, and the floor of our little garret is almost covered. Love to all.

Yours affectionately,
E.C.

My Dear Charlotte,

We have been in a dreadful state within the week, from the heavy rain &, and the contest between us and the store-closet has now ended in our defeat. I have been obliged to move almost everything out of it, and leave it to splash itself as it likes until it can be mended. Would that my pen could flow as fast as the rain in the store-closet. However I will do my best and tell you that we played a pool of Commerce with the Holders and, in spite of my disinclination to do so, I walked for a while beside the Cobb with Miss West. She would not actually mount the steps up onto the Cobb, avowing that the wind was too strong, and, although she knew it was a foolish fancy of hers, she was convinced that it would blow her into the sea. I felt that this remark deserved no answer so I asked after her mother.

"Poor mama is not well, she has the colic. I fear it may be something she ate that disagreed with her."

"Have you consulted Dr King?" I asked.

"Oh no, mama has no opinion of medical men. She prefers to prescribe for herself."

"Of course, you told me that she has a great knowledge of herbs and medicines. Has she carried a stock of them with her from Kent?"

"Oh yes, she never travels without them. Mama says one never can tell when they may be needed."

"Indeed." We walked in silence for a while and then Miss West said "Miss Cowper, do you not think that Mr Rivers is a very agreeable man?"

As you may imagine, I was somewhat startled by this question. "Very agreeable," I said. "Indeed, it is universally acknowledged that Mr Rivers is a gentleman of charm and affability and a great asset to our society. Do you have a special reason for thinking so?"

She looked confused. "No—no particular reason. It is just that he has called upon us several times."

"Really?"

"I was not sure—his attentions have been quite marked, mama has said so."

"And she is displeased?"

"Oh no—indeed she seems almost to encourage him. But I am not sure I should do so since I am engaged to Mr Russell."

So Mrs West is hoping to bring James Russell forward by making him jealous. I suppose it may work.

"I am sure," I said, "your mama knows best."

As you can imagine, I await the next episode of this little drama with great interest. I still have not decided whether to tell Sir Edward about the engagement—if such it be, but, in the light of his suspicions of Mr Rivers, I most certainly will tell him of Mrs West's skills, so that he may understand that Mr Rivers is not the only person in our small circle with a knowledge of herbs and medicines.

Since Sir Edward's boys are to come tomorrow I have been busy searching the schoolroom for Frank's 'collection' and have discovered many other treasures while I was about it. That ivory pen, curiously carved, that we fell out about ten years ago found itself at the back of the drawer of the old dresser in the corner, along with a shrivelled skeleton of some small creature, which I presume to be one of William's specimens. I will include the latter, since boys are interested in such things. The pen, however, I will claim for myself, since, you will recall, it was originally a present to *me* from old Mrs Woodward and not to you as you claimed at the time. I do not wish to open old quarrels but I think, with the passing of time and with mature reflection, you will admit the justice of my cause.

Our mother has asked that the boys should come on their own, merely delivered by Miss Blair, since she would have them freed from the restriction of their governess—though I, myself, have never observed any such restriction!

Rugeley conveys to us a third volume of sermons from Hamstall, just published, and which we are to like better than the two others; they are professedly practical and for the use of country congregations.

We heard yesterday from Frank whose complaints about the tediousness of the business in Vienna seem to have been modified somewhat by the presence of a Miss Forsyth. He was introduced to her at a formal dinner and then encountered her at a ball a few days later and seems to have been greatly struck by her wit and beauty. It would seem that she will be in Vienna for some time since her father, Sir Stuart Forsyth, is on a mission there and has had the forethought to bring his wife and daughter with him. As you may imagine, our mother is in raptures and can scarcely talk of anything else and is extremely annoyed with Frank for not providing the many and more particular details she wishes for. Poor Miss Forsyth, she little knows what expectations she has raised!

Your affectionate sister,
E.C.

I may now inform you that the store cupboard, I hope, will never trouble us again, for much of the evil is proved to have proceeded from the gutter being choked up, and we have had it cleared.

My Dear Charlotte,

We have now had the visit of Sir Edward's boys which I think may be considered a success. They were in raptures at Frank's collection and determined to make one of their own, questioning me closely as to where the best specimens might be found. The skeleton, pronounced by George to be that of a weasel, was greatly admired and I had no hesitation in bestowing it upon him. I scarcely think William will grieve for its loss. Our father coming in while they were here, took them with him to visit Bates at the farm, an action much approved of by our mother.

"Poor little souls," she said, "since their mother died and with their father abroad they have been left to servants and governesses, and now they are living in that dismal house! If you remember, Sir Edward's brother, who died and left it to him, was never married and hardly ever entertained, scarcely saw anyone except on business—no wonder everything there is so melancholy for the boys! It occurs to me, Elinor, for their next visit, you might look out the battledore and shuttlecock that you all used to play with."

To our surprise Sir Edward himself arrived to take the boys home. However, our mother insisted on their finishing the jellies and cheesecakes that she had provided before they went, and left the drawing room to oversee the feast.

"It is remarkably kind of your mother—and, indeed, of you, Miss Cowper, to take such trouble with them," he said.

"My mother enjoys having children about the house again."

"Are there no grandchildren?"

"My two brothers are abroad and have not yet married. My sister Mary's children are not of an age to make the journey on their own—my sister finds that travel disagrees with her."

"It is very good of you to entertain the boys. I am conscious that they need to be more in the world before they go away to school. I am truly grateful for the trouble you have taken."

"It is no trouble, I assure you. They are charming boys and, as I believe I have mentioned before, it is a pleasure to me to revisit the pastimes of my youth. My sister Charlotte frequently had to reprove me for joining in my brothers' games, an activity she found unladylike and which she maintained would unfit me for polite society."

"I am delighted to observe that she was wrong."

A compliment! But, then he was obliged to be civil after I had been entertaining his sons.

I thought it wise to change the subject and told him of Mrs West's talents with herbs and medicines.

"So you see, sir, Mr Rivers is not the only person in Lyme who has knowledge of such remedies."

"Indeed. That is interesting. But, interesting as it is, it does not really forward the investigation, for I cannot conceive of any reason why Mrs West might want to dispose of Mrs Woodstock."

So you see, My Dear Charlotte, what a quandary I found myself in! After a moment's hesitation I decided that there was nothing for it but to tell him everything, since otherwise he would think my information about Mrs West foolish and irrelevant, and, besides, at this particular moment, considering himself in my debt, he might not view my lack of candour too severely.

"Sir Edward, I fear I have been less than open with you. There are circumstances which might make it possible for Mrs West to wish for Mrs Woodstock's removal."

"Indeed?"

"I did not tell you before because it would have meant betraying a confidence..."

"I see."

Somewhat daunted by his severe expression, I nevertheless continued, "Miss West informed me (in the greatest secrecy) that she has been engaged to Mr Russell for some months, but, dependent as he was on his aunt's good will and in the knowledge that she would not approve, the engagement was not made public."

"Was there any reason why Mrs Woodstock should not approve of this engagement?"

"She would not have thought Miss West a suitable match for her nephew. Besides, she had other plans for him."

"But, now, even though his aunt is dead, he has not acknowledged the engagement?"

"No. I imagine he feels it would be unsuitable at the present moment."

"And it might give others a reason to suppose her death welcome to him. I see." He was thoughtful for a moment and then he said "I am obliged to you, Miss Cowper, for deciding to take me into your confidence in this matter—even at this late date."

I was about to speak, to defend my tardiness, when our mother came back into the room with the boys who besieged their father with exclamations of pleasure about the specimens and about their trip to the farm where there had been a litter of ferrets which they were anxious to acquire. He silenced them quickly and with renewed expressions of gratitude to our mother and a stiff bow to me, made his departure.

So now, I suppose I am in disgrace with Sir Edward Hampton, Magistrate. But, really he can hardly have expected me to break my word to Miss West, who had most earnestly sworn me to secrecy. I wish now that I had not told him of it.

I am glad that your visit to Mary is coming to an end so that you can see for yourself how things are going on here. I am sure you will feel as I do that Sir Edward is taking the whole affair too seriously. Indeed, I begin to wonder if Mrs Woodstock did not die a completely natural death and that the whole business is not just a self-important interference on the part of Sir Matthew and an excess of zeal on the part of Sir Edward.

Mary never sent her love to me in your last letter, but I send her mine and am

Your affectionate sister,
E.C.

My Dear Charlotte,

Your letter was a shock to us all. Having looked forward so much to your return in the immediate future it was a particular disappointment to find that this was not to be. We understand that, given our uncle's illness, our aunt has expressed a strong wish for your company. You say that this attack was particularly strong and, although the medical opinion is that his position is not grave, I do see that our aunt's agitation at his condition might make your attendance on her necessary, and I do believe that there is no-one who could be of more comfort to her at this time. You say that you owe her a special duty since she took such trouble for your entertainment when you were in Bath, but while this is true, it must be said that the desire for entertainment is strong in her own nature. So we must hope that our uncle will rapidly improve so that you may both enjoy the pleasures of the town, and with that thought I will try to bear with patience the delay of your return.

I am glad to hear that they are sending the carriage to convey you to Sloane St., and agree with Mary that it was the least they could do!

I spent Friday evening with the Mapletons, lately come into the district, and was obliged to submit to being pleased in spite of my inclination. It was a good dinner; amongst other things we had a fine lobster, which made me wish for you. Of the daughters, Marianne is sensible and intelligent; and Jane, considering how fair she is, is not unpleasant. A Mrs Gould was of our party with her son and they brought me home in their carriage. He is a very young man, just entered Oxford, wears spectacles, and has heard that 'Evelina' was written by Dr Johnson.

We hear that Mr Russell has gone to London again so I was not surprised to see Miss West walking along the Parade with Mr Rivers. He seemed most attentive and she was looking particularly fine in a blue velvet mantle and a bonnet of matching silk, elegantly covered with crape. They were much occupied with each other's conversation and did not see me so I was able to observe them at my leisure. It may be that

Mrs West regards him as a second string to her bow and would, perhaps, consider queening it with her daughter in Barbados.

We are reading "Clarentine" and are surprised to find how foolish it is. I remember liking it much less on a second reading than at the first, and it does not bear a third at all. It is full of unnatural conduct and forced difficulties, without striking merit of any kind.

There is a chill in the air and we have had fires these last few days. I am out of sorts from disappointment at your not coming and have no other news to fill up the sheet. I hope this reaches you before you leave. Please let us know, as soon as you arrive, what state our uncle is in.

Your affectionate sister
E.C.

Tell Mary that a hamper of apples has also been sent her from Kintbury so she may not begrudge us ours!

My Dear Charlotte,

We were much relieved to hear that you had arrived safely at Sloane St and that our uncle's condition has much improved. Certainly if you are obliged to be in London, then this is a good time to be there now that the town is once again full of company.

You ask whether I have had further conversation with Sir Edward. It happened that he was passing when I came out of Rugeley's bookshop—he has not yet obtained for us the second volume of Espriella's Letters that our mother ordered—and, though I would have bowed and passed on, he obviously wished to speak to me.

"Miss Cowper," he said "I fear I was not civil to you when last we met. It was perfectly natural that you felt you could not easily break a confidence and I do understand and apologize."

"No, indeed, sir, it is I who should apologize. In such a matter, a question of *law,* it was foolish of me to withhold information that might well be important to you."

"I do believe that it might be. Certainly, if Mrs Woodstock would oppose the marriage, then Mrs West and her daughter had reason to wish her away. But since they were obviously not on terms with the Woodstocks, the difficulty would lie in how they might gain access to the household."

"That would not be difficult since, whether by accident or design, their maid, Deborah, has made friends with the cook at Holcombe and is often in the kitchen there. If Mrs Woodstock's syllabub was prepared beforehand then she might well have been in a position to meddle with it."

He nodded approvingly. "So you, too, considered the syllabub. It certainly occurred to me that it might well have been the source of Mrs Woodstock's death. Is there any way we might discover whether the dish in question might have been left exposed to temptation?"

Accepting the 'we' as a sign that my opinion was once again required, I said, "Lucy, one of our servants, has a sister who works at Holcombe. I will ask her—in a roundabout way of course—to see what the arrangements were."

123

He gave that half smile I have remarked upon before, and said "You are a diplomat, Miss Cowper, like your brother."

"Indeed, sir, I do not believe Frank would agree with you. He—and William, as well as my sister Charlotte—have frequently reproved me for speaking in too forthright a fashion."

"There is also a place for candid speaking, though I fear it is not very often that one of your sex is allowed to indulge in it. But what news of your brother? Your father tells me he is in Vienna. Does he find that the negotiations progress?"

"I believe he is concerned at the tardiness of affairs there and the general level of confusion, which I suppose, is only to be expected when several nations are called upon to agree a plan that affects each one differently."

"Very acute, Miss Cowper," he said and continued to speak of the negotiations with considerable knowledge and clarity so that I understood for the first time some of the complexities of the affair. Indeed, our conversation continued for so long that I found we had arrived at the end of Broad St, by the Assembly Rooms, a direction I had not, in fact, intended to take and which meant that I had a much longer walk home than I had anticipated, and when I arrived back I recollected that I had forgotten to order the soles for tomorrow from Parker down at the Cobb.

Walking along the Parade, before I went to Rugeley's I met Mrs Holder in a new black velvet pelisse lined with yellow and a white bobbin net veil, and looking remarkably well in them. The orange wine—you will remember we made some from those oranges from Seville that our mother had the receipt for—will want our care soon. Though that will mean nothing to you, who will be eating ices and drinking French wine and above such vulgar economy.

Love to our aunt and hoping for news of our uncle's better health

Yours affectionately,
E.C.

My Dear Charlotte,

I was delighted to have your reply so soon and with good news of our uncle. I feel the fact that our aunt proposes to take you to the collection of Sir Joshua Reynold's paintings in Pall Mall is a sign that the immediate cause for concern is over.

You say that you are glad that I am now back on terms with Sir Edward. Certainly it is more comfortable, especially in such a small society as ours, not to be at odds with *anyone*. I did get from Lucy the information that Cook always made Mrs Woodstock's syllabub first thing, early in the morning, and that Deb was in the kitchen at Holcombe that very day, whether for her own entertainment or at her mistress's request I do not know.

Mr Russell is returned from London. He was in attendance on his uncle when our mother and I paid Mr Woodstock a visit yesterday. It seemed to me that he was at pains to be especially affable, waiting upon his uncle as assiduously as he once did upon his aunt and quite deposing Mr Rivers as chief attendant.

"So you are back from London," our mother said to him, "and are you fixed in Lyme this time?"

"For a long time I hope," he replied. "I am always most happy to be here, and have only left to attend to certain matters of business, nothing else would have taken me away from my uncle at such a time."

"James has been most helpful," Mr Woodstock said "seeing to everything for me here. I was especially grateful to him since Dr King said that any exertion on my part might have serious consequences on my health after such a dreadful shock to the system."

We did not stay long since Mr Russell reminded his uncle that they were to go for a short drive in the barouche.

"Dr King believes that a little gentle exercise would be beneficial," Mr Woodstock said, "and, provided that the weather is sufficiently mild—as James assures me it is to-day—then the sea air can be most favourable to one's health."

At that point Chapman came in laden with cloaks and shawls so we left. Later that day I met Mr Rivers leaving Mrs West's lodgings. Since we were walking in the same direction we fell into conversation.

"I have just been leaving tickets for the concert at the Assembly Rooms for Mrs West and her daughter. Mr Woodstock is a subscriber and, since neither he nor James wishes to attend I thought that they might care to use them. Being newcomers to the town they do not have the benefit of being on the subscription list and Miss West is very fond of music."

"Really?"

"Indeed she plays beautifully—though the instrument in their lodgings is inferior, quite unworthy of her talents—and has the most charming voice. She is very modest about her gifts but her mother persuaded her to give us some fine old Scottish airs."

"And you, sir, are also fond of music?"

"In our limited circle in Barbados, as you may imagine, it is one of our greatest pleasures to give small impromptu concerts when we are gathered together."

"It sounds delightful. And when will you be returning there?"

"That I am not at able to say at present. There are many matters of business to be arranged before I go back and my cousin has not yet recovered sufficiently from the dreadful events that have left him still in great distress."

"I am sure, sir, that your many friends in Lyme will be happy to hear you are to remain for a while."

"People have been most kind. Mrs West, for instance, whom, at first, I took to be somewhat reserved, is most affable and Mr and Mrs Chamberlyne as well as your amiable parents have all made me most welcome."

So you see, My Dear Charlotte, Mrs West is decidedly encouraging him. And a thought has occurred to me that, if she herself is not responsible for Mrs Woodstock's death, she may suspect that it may have been Mr Russell who did the deed. So, since she would hardly wish her daughter to form an alliance with a murderer (certainly not one who might well be discovered), then she is holding Mr Rivers in reserve, as it were, in case this may be so.

Our weather I fancy has been just like yours; we have had *some* very delightful days, our 11th and 12th were what the 11th and 12th of October should always be, but we have always wanted a fire within doors at least, except for just the middle of the day. We had a hare and a pheasant the other day from Sir Thomas Egerton so our larder is now very rich.

Your affectionate sister,
E.C.

19th October

My Dear Charlotte,

I was delighted to learn that our uncle is now making progress so that you were able to accompany our aunt when she went to Wedgwood's to choose a dinner-set. The pattern of a small lozenge in purple, between lines of narrow gold, with a crest, sounds very fine and will, I imagine, grace some splendid dinner-party very soon.

Our own domestic news is less grand. Our father has had the particulars of the building, etc and seems well satisfied. A narrow door to the pantry is the only subject of solicitude; it is certainly just the door which should not be narrow, on account of the trays; but if a case of necessity, it must be borne

Sir Edward called this morning to see our father—something about the shooting prospects for the season—and I was able to have a brief word to inform him about Deb's presence in the kitchen at Holcombe when the syllabub had already been prepared. Wishing to confirm my new resolution of candour, I also gave him the news of Mr Rivers being received so cordially by Mrs West and my thoughts on the reason for it.

"That is, to be sure, an interesting theory and one which a mere man would not immediately have perceived," he said. "No, seriously, Miss Cowper, it is just such observations that may be of great value and an excellent reason for my having asked your father if you and Mrs Cowper might assist me in this way."

"It may all be nonsense, of course," I said "but Mrs West does seem to me the kind of person who will not let any opportunity slip by her, whether it be of immediate use or no."

"And do you think Mr Russell the likeliest person to have killed Mrs Woodstock?"

"Put in those particular words, sir, I would hesitate to say so. It is difficult, you will admit, to consider any person of one's actual acquaintance capable of such a deed."

"But looked at dispassionately, Miss Cowper, and I am sure that, unlike many members of your sex, or indeed my own, you are able to view things dispassionately, do you think that Mr Russell has the strongest reason to do such a thing?"

"Viewing the affair in that particular way, sir, I must confess that I do find him the person who had most to gain from his aunt's death."

"But?"

"But I would doubt his resolution to carry out such a deed. He has always seemed to me to be a very shallow young man, ineffectual, you might say, the sort of person who might think of a daring stroke but who would lack the confidence or the courage to carry it through."

"As I have had reason to say before, your powers of observation are most acute. Indeed, I am grateful that I may never learn your summary of *my* character! But I am glad to have a clearer picture of Mr Russell's and it does confirm what I have been able to gather for myself in our brief acquaintance. Nevertheless I will discreetly inquire into his doings and see what may be found. And, we must not forget that, apart from Mr Woodstock, he was the only other person who dined with Mrs Woodstock on that day."

At that moment our father came in and carried Sir Edward off to see a gun he thought of buying. But you will see that I am reinstated in my position as Assistant Magistrate, something I do find sufficiently amusing to provide me with entertainment while you are enjoying the pleasures of the town.

I almost forgot to say that there was another letter from Frank, but our mother was disappointed in it since it was addressed to our father and contained only his view of affairs in Vienna and had not even the most fleeting reference to the beautiful Miss Forsyth. There is no news of his coming home, however, so our mother is still in hopes that *something* may come of it. I was sorry our mother had not the interest she hoped for, since for a day or two she was poorly with a return of her old complaint, but it did not last for long and seems to have left nothing behind it. She is now quite as well as one can expect her to be in weather which, although not severe, deprives her of exercise. She sends her love to you all as I do.

Yours affectionately,

E.C.

My Dear Charlotte,

I am delighted that you have kept up your old habits of correspondence even though you are leading such a busy life in Sloane St. I was glad that you were able to go to Belgrave Chapel on Sunday morning, though sorry that you were prevented by rain from going to the evening service at St James. Your more worldly activities continue to provide me with much food for envy. The shopping, especially, makes me feel the lack of having any but Layton's to visit here in Lyme. I was astonished that you had to go early to Grafton House to be sure of getting immediate attendance, and I feel that six shillings was a large sum to pay for a white silk handkerchief, but if you purchased it at Crook and Besford's in Pall Mall, then I suppose that was not out of the way. It was very kind in our aunt to make you a present of it.

There was a thorough party at the Chamberlynes the other evening; a commerce table and music and dancing in the other room. There were two pools at commerce, but I would not play more than one, for I could not afford to lose twice in an evening. Both Mr Russell and Mr Rivers were invited, but Mrs Chamberlyne told our mother that Mr Russell had elected to stay at home with his uncle, who no longer ventures out in the evening. Mr Rivers, however, was there, as was Miss West who seemed in spirits, in spite of the absence of her fiancé. Of course, it may be that the cause of her contentment was the knowledge that in a rose-coloured gown of finest gauze she quite outshone any lady in the room, even Miss Woodward (hitherto our recognized Beauty), in purple with a great deal of bare shoulder and gold lace trimming. Miss West was dancing with Richard Cooke when Mr Rivers arrived and he stood at the side of the room until she was free and then, although, very properly, he was not dancing, he engaged her in conversation for some time and took her into supper, all with the seeming approval of her mama.

I am surprised, though, that Mr Rivers should have left his uncle to the company of Mr Russell, since Mrs Holder maintains that there is a rivalry between them for the attention of Mr Woodstock. Indeed, as she says, Mr Rivers is his own relation whereas Mr Russell is a connection only of his wife, and now that she is no longer here to enforce her wishes upon him, he may well consider the nearer ties of blood. In short, My Dear Charlotte, we have the makings of a very interesting state of affairs with the two young men at odds not only over a pretty face but also over the possibility of a pretty fortune!

Since you will wish to know, I wore my checked muslin with a band of the same round my head and I danced with Captain Tilson and Mr Cooke, when Miss West had done with him. He is a quiet young man who fancies himself a poet. And, since his mind was obviously elsewhere when dancing with me, he was probably composing verses to Miss West's beauty.

There was the same kind of supper as last time and the same want of chairs.

I am glad that our aunt's friends the Mortons have engaged themselves to take you about when she attends upon our uncle. From what you say, they sound most agreeable people. They were lucky to secure seats for Drury Lane, and in a front box, too, since, as you say, there is such a rage for seeing Kean. I greatly envy you seeing his Shylock.

Dame Bushell washes for us only one week more, after which time John Stevens' wife undertakes our purification. She does not look as if anything she touched would ever be clean, but who knows?

You say that black gauze cloaks are much worn. Do you intend to purchase one to wear at the theatre?

Your envious but affectionate sister,
E.C.

My Dear Charlotte,

I was greatly obliged to you for writing at once, in spite of all your engagements, to let me know about the Mortons' son and the intelligence he was able to give you. How fortunate that he should be acquainted with James Russell and so able to provide a thorough character of him. Obviously, we thought that, as a fashionable young man, he would have a great many expenses, but we assumed that his aunt kept him well supplied with money, since she enjoyed knowing that he was making a show in London. But the quantity of debts (many of them gambling debts) that you mention would have been beyond anything he might dare to mention to her. And, of course, gambling (not merely whist or commerce of course!) was something she had a horror of, after her uncle's excesses had brought misery to his family. You are right to say that I must tell Sir Edward of this if I can happen to meet with him.

From what you say, John Morton sounds a very pleasant young man and I certainly do not think a banker need necessarily be dull. According to our mother, our uncle, in his younger days, was very lively and it is only with the onset of age that he has taken to invalidism.

I was pleased to hear that he is to join the party when you go to the Somerset House Exhibition.

Later

I keep this letter open to let you know that I have seen Sir Edward and have given him your news of Mr Russell, which he seemed to think important. I saw him briefly in Rugeley's—he seems to be a constant customer there—when I was inquiring about a critique of Sir Walter Scott that Sir Thomas Egerton was telling me of. I was obliged to hurry away since our mother was waiting for me to go and call on the Chamberlynes.

Mrs Holder, who keeps an eye on such things, says that he (Mr Russell) is Mr Woodstock's constant companion, forever playing at cribbage or driving out with him. One thing is certain, he obviously does not think the time is ripe to inform his uncle of his entanglement with Miss West. Whether Mrs West will take steps in the matter, I do not know. I feel she would be loth to let such a prize escape her, though whether Mr Russell may be such a prize is now not certain.

Before I forget, our mother has desired me to ask you to purchase for her two bottles of lavender water, provided you should go to the shop on your own account, otherwise you may be sure she would not have you recollect the request.

I forgot to say that Mrs Chamberlyne told us that Mrs Estwick is married again to a Mr Sloane, a young man under age, without the knowledge of either family. He bears a good character however. She also said that she has heard from the Prices that they are *not* to have a house on Weyhill; for the present he has lodgings in Andover, and they are in view of a dwelling hereafter in Appleshaw, that village of wonderful elasticity, which stretches itself out for the reception of everybody who does not wish for a house on Speen Hill.

My thanks to you for the news about Mr Russell and my thanks also to young Mr Morton should you care to give them to him.

Yours affectionately,
E.C.

My Dear Charlotte,

It was indeed kind of the Mortons to take you to the play again. I was interested to hear of your having seen Miss O'Neal in 'Isabella' since we had all heard such good reports of it, but sorry to learn that, although she is a most elegant creature, she was not equal to your expectations. So I need not feel jealous, after all, of your good fortune.

Mr Russell has been seen by me going into the post office, perhaps to collect letters he does not wish his uncle to know of. I happened to be looking in the windows of Layton's when he emerged and he seemed confused when I greeted him and, indeed, he had several letters in his hand which he thrust into the pocket of his coat when he saw me. We exchanged views on the weather and he would have passed on but I felt I might take this opportunity to question him a little.

"And how is Mr Woodstock today?" I asked. "It seems to me that he has lately improved a little in spirits. It must be pleasant for him to have you and Mr Rivers to entertain him."

"Indeed, I do think he is better than he was."

"He talks of going to Bath; will you go with him?"

"I do not think it likely he will leave Lyme until this unhappy business is cleared up. But, of course, then I will happily attend on him in Bath."

"And will Mr Rivers go also; or will he have returned to Barbados?"

"I do not think he can stay away from Barbados for much longer."

"His business here about the Estate has been accomplished then?"

"Not yet. My uncle has been in no fit state to consider the plans he has."

"But you will advise him?"

"Naturally I will do whatever is in my power to help."

"Your aunt, I believe, had hitherto overseen his work there?"

"That is so, but, alas, she died before she had the opportunity to do so this time."

At that moment we both saw Mr Rivers walking with Miss West along the Parade. "Mr Rivers seems to be a great deal in Miss West's company," I said. "Do you think he may have intentions in that direction?"

For a moment he looked after them with an expression of extreme annoyance, but he recovered himself quickly and said, "I have no idea about Frederick's intentions, but I had the impression that he is still greatly attached to the memory of his late wife."

"Of course. But there is a son, is there not, do you not think he may wish to provide the boy with a mother?"

"It is possible, though they say that does not always answer, if there is not liking on both sides."

"No, perhaps Miss West is not the person to take on a ready-made family."

He did seem quite put out to see them together so perhaps he still retains his affection for her and may yet find the courage to speak to his uncle. What Miss West's thoughts may be in this matter I do not know. I cannot but feel she would be happier with Mr Rivers than with Mr Russell, even with his debts paid. But doubtless she will do as her mother wishes.

The masons are now repairing the chimney, which they found to be in such a state as to make it wonderful that it should have stood so long, and next to impossible that another violent wind should not blow it down.

I envy you your choice of shops and am very envious of what you say of the delightful caps in the shops in Cranbourne Alley

Yours affectionately,
E.C.

My Dear Charlotte,

Sir Edward came today, having left his boys at the farm to see the ferrets. "And I fear," he said, "they will not leave without one, and how will I face my keeper when I inform him they are his responsibility when the boys are gone to school?"

"Come, Sir Edward," our mother said "you cannot make me believe that you are afraid of your keeper."

"But I assure you, ma'am, the whole success of the shooting season depends upon Higgs, and if he is put out then all will be lost."

"You talk a great deal of nonsense, sir. Now bring the boys back here when they are done. Cook has just this morning made some macaroons..."

She went off into the kitchen to seek out what she could find for them.

"Your mother is very kind," Sir Edward said.

"It gives her pleasure, and, indeed, I feel you deserve some recompense for our having introduced your sons to the ferrets."

He smiled and then said, "I am glad of the opportunity of thanking you properly for your information about Mr Russell's finances."

"It was the merest good fortune that my sister was in the company of one who knew him. But I must assure you that Charlotte questioned him most discreetly. I am sure Mr Morton was not aware of the reasons for her questions."

"Yet another diplomat in the family."

"Oh Charlotte is the sensible one."

"Well, I am most grateful for her good sense in this matter. I am going to London shortly and hope to make further inquiries myself. Discreetly, of course."

"I believe he has not yet told his uncle of his financial position. I met him leaving the post office the other day and he had been collecting letters which I believe he did not wish anyone else to see since he appeared embarrassed when he saw me and seemed disinclined to make conversation."

"So you engaged him in conversation, Miss Cowper?"

"It seemed a good opportunity to do so when he was somewhat confused."

"Of course. And what did you glean from this conversation?"

"Certainly his dislike and jealousy of Mr Rivers. I am sure he fears him as a rival with both his uncle and with Miss West."

"Indeed?"

"Mr Rivers is in her company a great deal at present and Mrs West seems quite satisfied that he should be so."

"Mr Rivers does not seem to be in a hurry to return to Barbados?"

"Apparently not. He has plans for the estate there, I believe, that he wishes Mr Woodstock to approve."

"Mr Woodstock is active in this matter?"

"It would seem that he will have to be now that Mrs Woodstock is no longer there."

"*She* oversaw Mr Rivers' running of the estate?"

"Indeed, she and Mr Woodstock's man of business—but mostly Mrs Woodstock—dealt with it all."

"And had she seen these plans of Mr Rivers'?"

"No, since she died before she had the opportunity to do so. In fact, I can recall her telling him, just before she died, that she wanted to see his accounts. It was in public, at a ball in the Assembly Rooms, in front of everyone. Poor Mr Rivers was greatly mortified."

Our mother coming back into the room as I was telling Sir Edward this broke in, "Indeed, that was her way—poor Mr Rivers, we all felt for him! Such a vulgar thing to do, speaking of business at such a time and in the card room too, but Mr Rivers, in the most gentlemanly manner merely bowed and withdrew. He is a charming man and we will all feel the loss of him when he returns to Barbados. Though he may yet remain in England since Mr Woodstock is greatly attached to him and Mr Rivers waits upon him most attentively."

When Sir Edward returned with the boys—who were immediately taken off by our mother and regaled with delicacies—he asked, "Do you think Mr Woodstock will ask his nephew's advice about Mr Rivers' plans?"

"Certainly Mr Russell believes he will. You think he may hope to find something amiss there?"

"It would be convenient for him. Miss Cowper, I would be most grateful if you could contrive to discover what happens there." He paused for a moment and then said "I am aware that I should not ask you to do such a thing...."

"On the contrary, sir, anything that will add interest to my life is most welcome."

"You wish for *interest,* Miss Cowper?"

"Not in the general way of things, I think, but within my own circle, perhaps, a little interest, something out of the ordinary, is an agreeable addition to life."

"You are fortunate to be so contented."

"I see no point in being anything other. Indeed, by and large, I find sufficient to interest me in the people and places around me; my observations provide entertainment enough."

"I am most grateful for those observations. And now I must relieve your mother of my sons and that burdensome animal."

How delightful that you were in a private box at the theatre, thanks to friends of the Mortons, right on the stage and, as you say, much less fatiguing than in the common way. However I note that you did not leave Don Juan in hell until half-past eleven and yet were up early the next morning to go to Grafton House. I salute such energy!

Your affectionate sister,

E.C.

My Dear Charlotte,

I was pleased to hear that our uncle is now sufficiently re-covered to have attended service last Sunday at St James and later, to take advantage of the unseasonable mildness of the weather, to enjoy a short drive in the carriage. Does this im-provement mean that your return home may be hoped for soon? I do not have to tell you that you are greatly missed and asked for almost daily by our acquaintance here in Lyme.

Sir Edward will, by now be in London, and I hope his in-quiries may be fruitful as this business of Mrs Woodstock's death has now dragged on for so long that people no longer talk about it, considering it stale news. However, Mr Rivers is still here in Lyme and our mother says that to see him and Mr Russell both attending on Mr Woodstock puts her in mind of two dogs jealously guarding a bone. We called upon him yesterday and found the poor man in a state of some confusion. Mr Russell, it seems, had offered to help him consider Mr Rivers' plans for the estate in Barbados, which had annoyed that gentleman considerably. He implied that it was the con-cern only of Mr Woodstock and his man of business and that Mr Russell should not interfere—all of this couched in the politest tones, but very firmly expressed, and Mr Russell taking offence and protesting that his only wish was to assist his uncle and implying, on *his* part, that Mr Rivers might have something to hide. All of this we had got from Mrs Holder, who had happened to call when both young men were absent and poor Mr Woodstock was able to confide his problems to her.

I must tell you that you are likely to have a visit from Sir Edward at Sloane Street. It seems that he informed our mother that he was going to London and (purely as a matter of form I have no doubt) asked if she had any commissions for him while he was there. Our mother, inspired I am sure by your frequent references to Grafton House, seized the op-portunity to bestow upon him a letter to you with many instruc-tions about purchases she wants you to make (Layton's being so sadly lacking in everything one really desires) with the money for you to pay for them without appealing to our uncle for funds to do so. I imagine Sir Edward was somewhat dis-

141

composed (our mother denies this) at being taken so readily at his word, but was too gentlemanly to show it. Our mother's letter is even now, in Sir Edward's carriage, on its way to you. So you will have the opportunity (which you have frequently wished for in your letters) to form your own opinion of him.

Our father is doing all in his power to increase his income by planting the new crops throughout the estate and does not despair of getting very nearly two thousand a year.

Mr Foote (a cousin of Mrs Chamberlyne who was also present) dined with us on Friday and I fear will not soon venture again, for the strength of our dinner was a boiled leg of mutton, underdone even for Cook and Mr Foote (I later discovered) has a particular dislike of underdone mutton, but he was so good-humoured and pleasant that I did not much worry at his being starved. He gives us all the most cordial invitation to his house in the country.

While Sir Edward is away I determined to continue the 'investigation' on my own and have now learnt from Lucy (who got it from Sarah) that both Mr Rivers and Mr Russell were in the kitchen at Holcombe at some time during the day that Mrs Woodstock died and while the fatal syllabub (if such it was) had been made and was set aside on the dresser. Mr Rivers has the habit of going through the kitchen to get to the stables—a perfectly reasonable route to take. Mr Russell was sent down by his aunt to see why the bell in the Library had not been answered, which also bears the ring of truth. I do not think it would have been difficult for either of the two gentlemen to add some noxious substance to the syllabub since there is always (so Lucy says) so much going on in the kitchen that any one action might very well pass unremarked.

Whether this information is of any use I do not know. Certainly it is likely that suspicion would rest most strongly on these two persons, and although there is much wickedness in the world, it is difficult to think that any person one has actually conversed with might be capable of such a deed.

Bates informed our father that the tinkers are in the neighbourhood again, so your chickens will be secured at night with especial care. Excuse the shortness of this, but I must finish it now, that I may save you an extra 6*d*.

Yours affectionately,
E.C.

My Dear Charlotte,

I was not entirely surprised to receive a letter from you so quickly since I was sure that you would be eager to let me know your opinion of Sir Edward! He certainly called upon you very promptly on his arrival in London. I would by no means call him handsome, though his appearance is good, I admit, for someone of his age, and his manners can be pleasing when he so wishes. I was surprised to learn that he proposes bringing back the purchases you are making for our mother since they could very easily have gone by carrier, and I can see why our uncle should have wished to include him in your theatre party by way of thanking him for his good offices.

You say that although our uncle's health is greatly improved, his doctor does not yet think him quite recovered and says his stomach is still rather deranged, and is keeping him in rhubarb and giving him plenty of port and water. So our aunt declares that she cannot do without you, and I suppose we must reconcile ourselves to your longer absence. At least we may imagine you in a continuous round of pleasure which (to our nobler natures) must give us great satisfaction though, of course, to you it must be nothing short of a genuine sacrifice!

The weather has been very cold, and yesterday I went with Miss Blair to watch the boys skating on the pond in the meadow by the beech. I hope the frost will hold for their sake. Our mother obliged me to look out the skates that Frank and William used when they were small and which she has been keeping these many years for little Charlie's use when he should be old enough. Afterwards we all came back home, at our mother's request, for hot soup and of course tarts for the boys. Miss Blair was nervous, at first, about the boys skating but our mother assured her (on no good grounds that I know of) that Sir Edward would wish them to do so. Miss Blair now looks upon our mother as the fount of all wisdom, not least because she (our mother) has found an excellent situation, when the boys go away to school, for her (Miss Blair) with the Goodwins—you may remember them as an amiable family with two small daughters—in Clifton. Miss Blair is delighted since she has a sister who teaches at a school in Bristol. Whether

Sir Edward will be content to have his household rearranged in this way I do not know—it will be a test of his good nature to see how he reacts!

I have passed on to our mother the news that there was but two yards of the dark slate poplin (at 4s a yard) but that the man at Grafton House promised to match it and send it off correctly. She thinks the stockings you bought at Remingtons were a bargain at 12s for the silk and 4s.3d for the cotton. The edging sounds very cheap and the plaiting lace at 3s.4d. I will write and tell Mary (since I owe her a letter) that there was no second set of Hook's Lessons for Beginners, and that you therefore have chosen her a set by another composer since you thought she would rather have something than not and that it cost 6s. Whether this will satisfy her I cannot tell, but she must admit that your intention was good!

Mr Russell continues suspicious of Mr Rivers and it is amusing to watch them each trying to out-do the other in their attentions towards poor Mr Woodstock who sometimes looks quite overwhelmed by their efforts. Lucy says that Sarah and the other maids are united in their dislike of Mr Russell's valet Corbett, a most disagreeable young man, who gives himself airs and demands the first cut of meat for dinner and other privileges because of his master's position in the household. Fortunately Chapman, who has a sharp tongue, has several times put him in his place, implying that Mr Russell may not be the favoured nephew much longer. All of which, Lucy says, makes life in the kitchen at Holcombe a disagreeable place, which must reflect on Mr Woodstock's comfort, for, as you know, such comfort depends to a degree upon the harmony prevailing among the domestics.

I have been looking over "Self Control" again, and my opinion is confirmed of its being an excellently meant, elegantly written work, without anything of nature or probability in it. I declare I do not know whether Laura's passage down the American river is not the most natural, possible, everyday thing she ever does.

No morning service today, wherefore I am writing this between twelve and one o'clock. Mr Rivers comes this afternoon if there be not snow, which by the look of things may be coming soon.

Your affectionate sister,
E.C.

My Dear Charlotte,

The snow, which did arrive, did not prevent Mr Rivers from calling upon us. He seemed in high spirits and was very full of information concerning Mr Woodstock's health and well-being. It seems that Mr Russell has been absent again for a few days and Mr Rivers has obviously wished to profit from this absence to extend his influence over his cousin.

"How fortunate," our mother said, "that Mr Woodstock has you to tend him when Mr Russell is away so often. In the winter, too, when those not in the best of health—and poor Mr Woodstock is certainly among that number—are most likely to be unwell."

"Indeed, madam," he said earnestly, "yesterday I was so anxious about him—his appetite was bad and he complained of a headache—that I sent for Dr King." Our mother nodded approvingly. "Dr King said that it was not a serious malady and gave him a dose of calomel, which seemed to do him good, but said he should keep to his bed for the remainder of the day."

"Very wise. Some people say that Dr King is over cautious, but I believe that to err on the side of caution has saved many lives and Dr King agrees with me. Mr Woodstock is not strong—his nerves are easily agitated—and that sort of person can very easily succumb to any kind of illness in the neighbourhood. Indeed poor Mr Mildmay had a bad case of colic only last week and Maria Brompton a very unpleasant cold and sore throat. So, you see, one cannot be too careful in such matters and Mr Woodstock is very lucky that you are there to look after him. But tell me, what was so urgent that Mr Russell had to leave his uncle?"

"He said it was a matter of business, but what sort of business I cannot say."

"Business for his uncle?"

"His own business—certainly it required him to go to London for several days."

"Well, I suppose young men will find any excuse for going up to enjoy the pleasures of London. But you, Mr Rivers, do you not find Lyme very dull?"

149

"Indeed no, ma'am. It is delightful to me to be in England once again and I am particularly happy to be in such a charming place as Lyme and in such pleasant company."

"Well, you must settle here. I am sure you will be happier in Lyme than in Barbados—though I am sure it is very agreeable—and we would all be most pleased if you were to remain here."

"Alas, I have my way to make in the world and must go back to Barbados quite soon to attend to business there."

"Oh I am sure your cousin will think you too valuable to let you go back; he will surely find much to do to keep you here."

He smiled but made no reply, though I do believe that he would much prefer to stay in Lyme where he can continue to pursue Miss West.

The snow having melted the following day we had a very pleasant time at Ashe, we sat down fourteen to dinner in the study, the dining room being not habitable from the storms having blown down *their* chimney. Mrs Bramston talked a good deal of nonsense, which Mr Bramston and Mr Clerk seemed almost equally to enjoy. There was whist and a casino table, and six outsiders. Rice and Lucy flirted, Mat Robinson fell asleep, James and Mrs Augusta alternately read Dr Finnis' pamphlet on the cow-pox, and I bestowed my company by turns on all.

I was astonished to hear that when you were at the theatre you saw Mr Russell in another of the boxes and that Sir Edward seemed particularly interested in the company he was with. Since Mr Russell was in the audience, I was amused that the play was "The Hypocrite," from Moliere's "Tartuffe." I am sorry for your disappointment in seeing Mrs Edwin as the heroine and not Mrs Siddons, though you say her performance was good, as well as those of Dowton and Mathews. Nevertheless, I am pleased that our uncle is to give you the opportunity to attend one of Mrs Siddons' public readings, which she is now chiefly engaged upon since her retirement from the theatre.

Mr Mildmay, whom I encountered one afternoon at Mrs Chamberlyne's, is becoming so deaf that they say he could not hear a cannon were it fired close to him; having no cannon at hand I was not able to make the experiment, but he is indeed extremely hard of hearing and I was obliged to speak very loud to get any response from him. You were enquired after very prettily, Mrs Peters surpassed the rest in her attentive recollection of you, inquired more into the length of your absence, and desired to be "remembered to you when I wrote next". Which duty I hereby fulfill.

Your affectionate sister,
E.C.

My Dear Charlotte,

Sir Edward returned from London earlier than we expected. He waited upon us this morning with the many packages you sent for our mother. She is delighted with the purchases you made on her behalf and quite approves of the blue bombazine which you added on your own account and says that it will make up admirably into a morning gown. Our mother was anxious for news of you, and questioned Sir Edward closely concerning the state of our uncle's health. He expressed his pleasure in meeting you and refused (most politely) to express an opinion on the health or otherwise of our uncle, merely stating that he seemed to be in excellent spirits at the theatre party and appeared to have a good appetite at the dinner beforehand.

I was able to have a little private conversation with him while our mother went to search for some ivory fish for a set of Speculation that she had promised the boys.

"Charlotte tells me that Mr Russell was at the theatre the evening you were there," I said, "and that you were most interested in the company he was with."

"I should have known that your sister would share your gifts of observation—I was, indeed, much struck by her thoughts on a variety of subjects and her good sense in pronouncing upon them. Yes, it would seem that Mr Russell's acquaintances have a doubtful reputation."

"Indeed?"

"Which leads me to believe (and other inquiries I was able to make confirm this) that he may well have substantial gambling debts—and may, even now, be attempting to repair his fortunes by further excesses at the tables."

"Foolish indeed!"

"Young men are often foolish, but I imagine Mr Russell allowed his debts to accumulate while his aunt was alive, thinking that she would relieve him."

"I do not believe she would have given him money if she had known they were gambling debts. As I think I informed you before, she had a horror of gaming since ruined her uncle and left his family in a much impoverished state. No, I am sure that was something he had to keep from her at all costs since she would have never given him another penny if she had found out."

"I see. But *Mr* Woodstock has no such objections?"

"I do not think so—unless he feels bound to respect his wife's opinions. But I imagine Mr Russell would not feel obliged to explain for what particular purpose he required the money."

"And you think Mr Woodstock will continue the payments that his wife made to her nephew?"

"I imagine so. Unless he becomes so reliant upon Mr Rivers that he no longer feels any obligation to support Mr Russell."

"That may very well be true. Thank you Miss Cowper for your thoughts, they are most valuable." Our mother coming back into the room we had no further conversation on this matter.

We are very much disposed to like our new maid, Susan; she knows nothing of the dairy, to be sure, which in our family is rather against her, but she is to be taught it all by Lucy. In short, we have, as you know, felt the inconvenience of being without a second maid so long, that we are determined to like her. As yet, she seems able to help Cook very well and says she can work well at her needle.

I am delighted to hear that you have been to a ball, and have danced at it, have supped with the Mortons, and that you should meditate the purchase of a new muslin gown. *I* am determined to buy a handsome one whenever I can, and am so tired and ashamed of half my present stock that I even blush at the sight of the wardrobe which contains them. But I will not be much longer libeled by the possession of my coarse spot; I shall turn it into a petticoat very soon.

I am very glad you recommended "Gisborne," for, having begun, I am pleased with it, and had quite determined not to read it.

Yours affectionately,
E.C.

My Dear Charlotte,

The most shocking thing has occurred. While walking in his uncle's covers yesterday Mr Russell was shot at and wounded. Mercifully the ball merely grazed his arm but I hear he bled profusely and could very well have been killed. The general opinion is that the miscreant is one of the tinkers, on Mr Woodstock's land, illegally shooting his game. Whoever it may have been, the whole town, as you may imagine, is in an uproar. Mr and Mrs Holder visited us this morning and could speak of nothing else.

"We could all be murdered in our beds!" Mrs Holder exclaimed. "That such a thing should happen at Lyme! Mr Holder went himself to see Sir Edward to inquire what was being done and Sir Edward merely said that the constable was looking into it, which is no answer at all when we are so anxious. We made a point of visiting Mr Woodstock this morning—poor man, he was in a great state and even Mr Rivers had much trouble in calming him."

Our mother asked, "Did you see Mr Russell himself?"

"No, he was keeping to his room."

"But he had seen Dr King of course?"

"No, he would not. He said it was a mere scratch and that his valet had attended to it."

"How foolish! Such a wound, if it be neglected, can lead to fever. Mr Woodstock must make him see Dr King."

"He would not, saying that it was a lot of fuss about nothing and Corbett was perfectly capable of dressing the wound. Well, you know how these young men are, not willing to show any kind of weakness."

"How did it happen?"

Mr Holder then took up the story. "The keeper is ill and, although Mr Woodstock does not shoot, he likes to know that everything is as it should be if either Mr Russell or Mr Rivers might wish to do so. Mr Russell offered to walk through the covers and see that all was well. He was quite a way inside the wood when he said he heard a rustling sound behind him, he half turned and then there was a shot and he found he was wounded."

"How dreadful!"

"He was, of course, not immediately in a condition to pursue his attacker and, indeed, as I hear, he was only just able to make his way back into the house."

"And his arm was badly wounded?" our mother inquired.

"There was certainly a great deal of blood which had soaked through the sleeve of his coat," Mr Holder said. His wife gave a faint scream at this unpleasant information but he continued, "He said it had grazed his left arm. A few inches to the right and it might well have pierced his heart."

"And Sir Edward has not done anything to find the attacker?" our mother asked.

"He has instructed the constable to make inquiries," Mr Holder said, "and he, himself, is to speak to Mr Russell today when it is hoped he will be in a fit state to see him."

So that is how matters stand and we all wait with eagerness and some anxiety to see what may happen next. As you may imagine, although we all enjoy any happenings out of the general way, such a violent event is beyond anything we may have thought of or, indeed, wished for. However, since the victim is Mr Russell, whom I do not care for, and since his injury was not fatal, I think I may indulge myself with being at least *intrigued* by this occurrence.

Yours affectionately,
E.C.

My Dear Charlotte,

When I was on my way home this morning I was approached in Church Street by Miss West, who was in a state of considerable agitation. "Miss Cowper, please tell me, how is Mr Russell? We have heard the most dreadful things! When my mother told me she had heard he had been shot I fainted quite away, and even now, as you may see, the terrible news has almost overcome me. Everyone seems to have a different story and I have no way of finding out the truth since, as you can imagine, it is not possible for me to make direct inquiries and I am quite frantic to discover how he is?" She grasped my arm. "He is not dead? Tell me he is not dead!"

"Pray do not agitate yourself, Miss West. Mr Russell is well, the injury was not dangerous—'a mere scratch' he called it."

She released my arm to clasp her hands together. "Oh how brave he is! But he is wounded?"

"The ball grazed his arm I believe."

"But he could have been killed! Oh that I might go to him!"

"He is very well looked after I assure you."

"Oh Miss Cowper, if only I could be as cold and rational as you, but I have a very sensitive nature and I feel things more than most people—and *such* a thing to have happened!" Since I made no reply—and indeed what reply could I make?—she continued in a more natural tone, "But do they know who has done this thing? Who could have wished to harm him?"

"It is thought that tinkers, shooting in the woods, shot him by mistake."

"Oh." She seemed downcast at such a prosaic answer but said, "But it may yet be proved otherwise. No-one has been taken up yet?"

"The constable is looking into the matter and Sir Edward Hampton, who, as you know is the magistrate, is speaking to Mr Russell about it. But it must surely be the tinkers. I do not know of anyone who might wish Mr Russell harm."

She was silent for a moment and then said "Oh Miss Cowper if only *I* have not been the cause of this dreadful thing!"

"You?"

"I had no idea that he felt so strongly!"

"Who?"

She opened her eyes very wide in that tiresome way she has and said "Mr Rivers of course."

"Mr Rivers? I believe he and Mr Russell are not on very friendly terms, being in some way rivals for Mr Woodstock's attention, but I know of no reason why he should wish to harm him."

"It is not only Mr Woodstock's attention they are rivals for" she declared dramatically.

"Indeed?"

"Mr Rivers has made me a declaration."

"A declaration?"

"He wishes to marry me," she said impatiently. "Of course, he had no idea of my attachment to Mr Russell—he is the soul of honour and would never have approached me if he had known I was promised to another."

"What did you tell him?" I asked, curious to know with what splendid equivocation she had answered him.

"I told him it was impossible since I was not free."

"And he accepted that?"

"Of course he tried to press me for more details, but I said I was bound to secrecy and could give him no answer."

"So he did not know that it was Mr Russell you are engaged to?"

She lowered her head. "He guessed," she murmured, "though it is not exactly an engagement..."

I wondered what Mrs West would have made of this admission.

"I see. So you think that Mr Rivers, maddened by jealousy, attempted to murder Mr Russell?"

She gave a little scream of protest "Oh Miss Cowper, I certainly did not say such a thing. Not *murder*—he may have wished to frighten Mr Russell so he that would go away, back to London. I could never forgive myself if *I* have been the cause of this terrible thing." She clutched my arm again. "Pray forget everything I have said—I could not bear anyone to know.... But he is well, you say, Mr Russell?"

"He is."

"Thank heavens. I must go—I have taken too much of your time, but you will understand that I *had* to know how he is."

So you see I was right about Mr Rivers' succumbing to Miss West's charms. Whether or not this passion so worked upon him that he felt compelled to rid the world of his hated rival (on two accounts) I do not know. I suppose it is possible, *man*kind being as it is, though I would not have thought Mr Rivers was one to discard prudence (and what could be more imprudent than shooting one's rival) for the sake of a pretty face. He always struck me as a sensible man, but who can tell to what lengths passion might drive one—or, at least, so the writers of fiction assure us.

What I would dearly like to know is what Mrs West makes of all this. I regret that, being so astonished at her news, I did not think to question her daughter on the matter. If Mrs West has somehow got news of Mr Russell's debts, she may well believe that Mr Rivers is a better match, however much Miss West may protest her devotion to Mr Russell. It may be, indeed, that the performance I witnessed in Church Street was set on by Mrs West to try to gather information which might assist her in making up her mind which suitor would be best pursued.

Since I was reproved for withholding information before, I will make a point of telling Sir Edward of this incident and see what he can make of it. Had I felt it was indeed a real confidence on Miss West's part I would hesitate to do so, having a certain delicacy about betraying (as you might say) a member of my own sex, but I cannot help feeling that I was, in some way, being made use of by Miss West or her mother and so have no qualms in doing so.

There is a new young woman in the neighbourhood who is making me a bonnet of the riding-hat shape; it will not be dear at a guinea. She is also making me a pelisse for 17*s;* she charges only 8*s* for the making, but the buttons seem expensive—*are* expensive, I might have said, for the fact is plain enough.

I rejoice at your activities and admire your energy—to the play again last night and out a great part of the morning shopping, and seeing the Indian jugglers. It was as well that the musical play "The Farmer's Wife" had only three acts so that you were home before ten.

We do not much like Mr Wilmot's sermons at present. They are full of regeneration and conversion, with the addition of his zeal in the cause of the Bible Society.

Yours affectionately,
E.C.

My Dear Charlotte,

Sir Edward, bringing his sons over to have instruction from Bates in the management of their ferret, called in to pay his respects to us and I was thus able to tell him of my encounter with Miss West. He was greatly interested and questioned me closely about my thoughts concerning Mr Rivers and his intentions. I was also able to give him intelligence which I had obtained from Lucy (which she had got from Sarah) that on the day Mr Russell was shot, Mr Rivers was absent on business for Mr Woodstock in Axminster. Nevertheless, John coachman told Sarah that he had seen Mr Rivers' horse tied up in the yard of the Crown Hotel that very afternoon. He would not be mistaken in the horse since it was he who persuaded Mr Woodstock to buy it from Captain Farrell when he was posted away from the district.

"That is, indeed, of some significance, Miss Cowper and I am most grateful to you for the information. I will be visiting Holcombe to have further conversation with Mr Russell, who would not say much when I spoke to him just after the incident. But I will use the occasion to question Mr Rivers also."

"Please, I beg you, do not mention that it was John coachman who spoke of it—it might get him into some trouble with his master if it were known."

"As always, Miss Cowper, you think of everything."

"You may laugh at me sir, but he has only just been re-instated since Mrs Woodstock's death and I am greatly concerned that nothing should cast doubt on his position, since he is to marry our maid's sister."

He smiled and said "I will be—what is the word?—discreet."

"Do you indeed think that Mr Rivers might have shot at Mr Russell?"

"It is possible, and one should never ignore the possible. If, as you tell me, he wishes to gain influence over his cousin he would be glad to be rid of Mr Russell now that Mrs Woodstock is no longer here to promote his interest. And, if he is also a rival for the hand of the beautiful Miss West..."

"But concerning Mrs Woodstock—surely he had no reason to wish her dead?"

"No reason presents itself, I admit, but I will make inquiries about him. I have a friend newly returned from Barbados and he may have some intelligence."

"And he *was* passing through the kitchen," I reminded him "when the syllabub had been made, as well as actually living in the house."

"Ah yes, the syllabub, we must not forget that."

Fortunately the boys returned before I could reply, full of their adventures with Bates and asking when they could come again. Our mother, I need hardly say, echoed their request. "And indeed, Sir Edward, we are always delighted to see them here. I have looked out several games for them which they greatly enjoy. They are such bright, intelligent boys. There are bilbocatch—John is quite indefatigable at that—and spillikins, paper ships, riddles, and conundrums." The boys responded with great joy to this invitation and Sir Edward promised that they should come later this week, which appeared to give great satisfaction to all concerned.

Yesterday we had the pleasure of receiving, unpacking and approving *our* Wedgwood ware which our aunt ordered for us. It all came very safely, and, upon the whole, is a good match. There was no bill with the goods, but that shall not screen them from being paid. Our mother means to ask our aunt to settle the account on our behalf. It will be quite in her way, for I believe she is just now sending us a breakfast-set from the same place.

I am happy to tell you that we have had a letter from Frank, saying that he hopes to be back in England before too long and plans, when his affairs in London are completed, to come down to Lyme. We are all, of course, delighted and our father suggested that, if you may be spared at Sloane Street, he might bring you back with him. As you can imagine, this met with our heartfelt approval—you have been away for far too long. Our mother, of course, professed herself delighted to have Frank back in the country, though she was, I felt, disappointed that he made no reference to the beautiful Miss Forsyth. I encouraged her to think that Sir Stuart Forsyth would almost certainly, by now, be back in London and his daughter with him.

We also heard from Mary today and she begs me to inquire of you whether they sell cloths for pelisses at Bedford House, and if they do, will be very much obliged to you to desire them to send her down patterns with the width and prices; they may go any day of the week from Charing Cross. Why she could not write to you herself about this matter I do not know, though, of course, I am always interested in her new purchases!

I greatly enjoy the exquisite weather we are having and selfishly hope we are to have it last till Christmas—nice, unwholesome, unseasonable, relaxing, close, muggy weather.

Yours affectionately,
E.C.

My Dear Charlotte,

The boys duly came and we played at spillikins and asked riddles and conundrums and were generally merry. "They are delightful boys," our mother said "and it makes me very sad to think that their mama died so young and had no chance to see them out of their babyhood. George is particularly inventive—did you see the design he drew for the footstool cover I am making? And John is so lively and engaging. I declare we shall be very dull when they go away to school and so I told Sir Edward. He is to get a tutor for them during the holidays (who should enter into their sports more than that poor Miss Blair) and, of course, their old nurse is still there to care for them, but it is a poor exchange for a mama to love them!"

Our ball at the Assembly Rooms was quite a success. There were more dancers than the room could conveniently hold, which is enough to constitute a good ball at any time. I wore my gauze gown, long sleeves and all, and danced most of the evening. There was one gentleman, an officer of the Cheshires, a very good-looking young man, who, I was told, wanted very much to be introduced to me; but as he did not want it quite enough to take much trouble in effecting it, we never could bring it about! One of my best actions was sitting down two dances in preference to having Lord Bolton's eldest son for my partner, who danced too ill to be endured. Neither Mr Russell nor Mr Rivers was present—nor even Sir Edward—so perhaps not having the interest of observing them made the evening, in spite of everything, seem rather flat. One incident, however, *was* remarkable. While her mother was in the card room, Miss West drew me to one side and, looking around to make sure we were not observed, said in some agitation "Oh Miss Cowper, I must speak with you—no, not here—tomorrow morning, by the Cobb at 11 o'clock. Please be there I beg of you, it is a matter of great urgency—do not fail me!"

You may well imagine how interested I was and, naturally, I was at the appointed place well before the time arranged, so that I was annoyed (though not, perhaps, surprised) when she kept me waiting for a full twenty minutes. However, when I saw her, I realised that it must have taken some time to have assembled such a delightful costume—a dark red velvet pelisse trimmed with fur, with a close bonnet, also trimmed with fur, in matching material with a pleated silk lining. I was glad to be wearing my new bonnet, of the riding hat shape that I told you of, to draw attention from my old blue kerseymere cloak. We ascended the Cobb and she began talking very quickly so that I had to strain to hear her words although it was a mild, still day with no wind.

"Oh Miss Cowper, I am so glad you came – I was so afraid you would not—so good of you—I am in such distress and there is no-one I can turn to."

"Pray compose yourself, Miss West and tell me what the matter is. Are you still concerned about Mr Russell?"

"No, no—that is not the matter—though it is to do with Mr Russell."

"Indeed?"

She stopped still and faced me. "I fear," she said earnestly "I have quite mistaken my feelings for him."

"I see. And you have not told him so?"

"Oh no, I dare not. My mother would be so angry; she is still of the opinion that Mr Russell will speak to Mr Woodstock about our—our arrangement."

"But you do not feel you could marry him?"

"Oh no, not now!"

"Am I to understand that he has been supplanted in your affections by another?" (You will see, My Dear Charlotte, how easily one slips into this kind of high-flown language in such a case).

She bowed her head. "Oh it is too true!"

"And Mr Rivers—for I imagine it is he—returns your feelings?"

"Oh yes—indeed, Miss Cowper—that is what I want to consult you about—he wants us to elope together."

"What!"

"I know it is very shocking, but what else can we do? My mother would never allow me to marry him—he has no fortune—and would not let me go and live in Barbados."

"I see."

"Mr Rivers—Frederick—says we may be married in London by special licence; he can arrange it all. Miss Cowper, what should I do?"

"My dear Miss West I cannot advise you; it is something you must decide for yourself. It would, of course, be wrong for you to be obliged to marry Mr Russell against your will. I am sure your mama would not expect you to do so. And if *not* marrying Mr Russell is your only reason for eloping with Mr Rivers, then I would certainly advise you against it."

"Oh no, I do truly care for Mr Rivers and I think I would like to live in Barbados, away from mama."

"When did Mr Rivers suggest you should leave?"

"Immediately—or, as soon as he has made arrangements."

"Could you not persuade your mama to consent to your marriage to Mr Rivers?"

"Oh no. Once mama has made up her mind there is no changing it."

"But, although he may not have a personal fortune, he has an excellent position in Barbados and I am sure Mr Woodstock would, in time, make some settlement upon him."

"We could not wait for that—Mr Rivers says he must return to Barbados almost immediately."

"Why is that?"

"Business—I do not rightly understand, but he says it is urgent and he wants me to go with him."

"I see."

"So what should I do? Please tell me—I have no-one else I can turn to!"

"My dear Miss West you must see that I cannot possibly make such a decision for you. You must think very hard before you commit yourself to a man you know very little of and a new life in a strange land."

"So you think I should refuse?"

"I think you should take thought before you decide."

"I suppose so—but it is so difficult."

"You will not tell Mr Rivers that you have consulted me?"

"Oh no, he was very anxious that I should tell no-one about it."

So you see, My Dear Charlotte, something most strange is in the wind, and if Mr Rivers is about to leave the country unexpectedly than I must somehow get a message to Sir Edward to let him know about it; perhaps he may discover what this *business* may be.

Yours affectionately,
E.C.

My Dear Charlotte,

By the greatest good chance I came upon Sir Edward in Rugeley's shop. (Rugeley did not have Lord Macartney's "Journal of the Embassy to China" which our father requested so I was obliged to take Southey's "Life of Nelson" in its stead along with Madame D'Arblay's "The Wanderer" for our mother).

"Sir Edward," I said, "I was very much hoping to see you!"

"Indeed?"

"That is—I have information I felt you should know of right away."

I told him what Miss West had said and he nodded.

"That confirms what I have already discovered about Mr Rivers. Come, Miss Cowper, let me escort you home and I will explain as we go." He kindly gathered up my volumes and we left the shop. "I believe," he said, "I told you that I wished to make some inquiries about Mr Rivers's activities in Barbados. A friend of mine, with extensive knowledge of the place and just back from there, told me that there had been a scandal regarding Mr Rivers' dealings on Mr Woodstock's estate—some sort of financial mismanagement. He was obliged to apply to his late wife's father to settle the matter, which the gentleman did for the sake of his grandson. But I believe that if Mr Woodstock—or, especially *Mrs* Woodstock had known of this his position there would have been in grave doubt."

"But he was full of talk about his plans for extending and improving the estate."

"That, I imagine, was to keep at bay awkward questions as long as possible."

"Certainly, as far as I can tell, no-one has yet examined the accounts he brought back."

"Precisely. With Mrs Woodstock no longer in charge (and it may be he was the cause of her death) the matter lay idle and he hoped, I think, that he would have gained Mr Woodstock's confidence enough to put off that examination for ever."

"So why would he need to go now?"

"As you may recollect, I went to Holcombe the other day and spoke with Mr Russell and Mr Rivers. Mr Russell had nothing more to add to his description of the shooting, but he did let fall the information that Mr Woodstock had asked him to look at the Barbados accounts, which he intended to do after he had returned from London—more business concerning his debts I imagine—sometime next week."

"So that is why Mr Rivers was so urgent in his appeal to Miss West!"

"Indeed."

"So what will you do now? Will you confront Mr Rivers with this new information?"

"I must be circumspect in the manner in which I approach him, but I am anxious lest he should slip away before I can do so. Also, since what you have told me about Miss West, I am now most concerned for her."

"And I suppose I may not warn her about Mr Rivers in case she should alert him. But she must not be allowed to go away with him since he might be a murderer!"

"It is a sorry business and must be considered carefully. In other circumstances I would, of course, consult Mr Woodstock, but unfortunately I do not think I am likely to get much help from him."

"His nerves?"

"Precisely, and it would only serve to warn Mr Rivers of my suspicions."

"Is there anything I can do?"

"Indeed, Miss Cowper, there is something only *you* can do. Please, I pray you, find an opportunity to speak with Miss West and persuade her—and I am sure you can be very persuasive—not to go away with Mr Rivers."

"I will do my best, sir. Indeed I could not settle it with my conscience to allow her to take such a step now that I know what manner of man Mr Rivers is, or may be—though, I will, of course, be careful not to alarm her so that she frightens him away."

I waited upon the Wests that afternoon and begged her company on a walk. Mrs West seemed surprised, as well she might since I had not previously shown any preference for Miss West's company. However, she graciously approved our outing and as soon as we were well clear of the house I spoke urgently. "Miss West, I have been thinking most carefully about what you told me when last we met, and I am convinced that it would be most imprudent for you to go away with Mr Rivers in such a manner. Think how it might affect your reputation and, indeed, how you would be received in Barbados if the truth about the matter should ever be known. I believe that the rules of Society there are even stricter than they are in England and your position would be most uncomfortable."

"Oh dear, I did not think of that."

"There are many things to think of, not least how distressed you mother would be."

"Indeed."

It seemed to me that Miss West was not greatly concerned about her mother's distress so I tried another tack. "Men are very selfish, are they not? I am sure that Mr Rivers has made arrangements for a special licence and a church where you may be married, but I doubt he will have thought of how you will be able to procure your bride-clothes."

"He did not say so."

"I am not surprised, men do not consider such things. But I am sure you would not wish—on such a day—to be married in everyday garments."

"Indeed I would not."

She spoke with some feeling and I took the opportunity to press home the point.

"It is such an *important* day, one that comes only once in your life, and I do believe it would be a great pity not to have a proper ceremony, and that, I am sure you agree, means white satin and lace veils. Think how they would become you! I am sure Mr Rivers would wish to see you looking so."

She seemed much struck with this. "What should I do? Mr Rivers—Frederick—spoke of great haste. There may not be time."

"I am sure he would not wish to deprive you of all that would make the day most memorable for you. If he *must* leave at once, say you will follow him and when he has settled his business then he may send for you and you may be married in a proper manner."

"He may not like this."

"Then you must be firm—after all, if he really cares for you he will quite understand how much all this means to your happiness. You may think of it as a test of his love."

"Indeed I will!"

So there I had to leave the matter. I trust that she is vain and silly enough to be swayed by my arguments, and I hope that Mr Rivers' situation is so urgent that he will give up all thoughts of taking her with him. Now I must find some way of letting Sir Edward know what I have done. I believe our father has invited him to shoot over our covers tomorrow so I will hope to find an opportunity of speaking with him without attracting too much notice.

I am delighted that you are making the most of your remaining time in London—"The Clandestine Marriage" and "Midas" at Covent Garden—how I envy you, though I suppose I might claim to have had a deal of drama (I might well say melodrama) here!

Your affectionate sister,
E.C.

My Dear Charlotte,

So Mr Rivers has gone—and without Miss West! Sir Edward came this morning to inform our father and we all heard his account of what had happened. It seems that Mr Rivers left at some time during the night—none of the servants stirring. He took with him the Barbados accounts and Mr Woodstock's second best horse. Whether the sale of the latter will be enough to provide for his passage to Barbados I do not know—if, indeed, he has sufficient effrontery to return there.

Sir Edward's assuring me that Mr Rivers had left alone, led to his explaining the part Miss West had played in the story. Our father did not quite like my part in the matter, but Sir Edward assured him that I had acted solely at *his* request and that my intervention had undoubtedly saved an innocent girl from possible ruin.

Mr Russell, it seems, was very loud in his condemnation of Mr Rivers and horrified (he said) at the way Mr Woodstock had been deceived. Now, of course, he will have the field to himself and I have no doubt his uncle will pay off all his debts.

"Do you think," I asked, "that Mr Rivers was the person responsible for the shooting? It would have suited him to have Mr Russell removed."

"It is possible."

"And," our father asked, "are we to assume that Mr Rivers was responsible for Mrs Woodstock's death?"

"That does seem probable. Though we may never know by what means he accomplished that end."

"The syllabub?" I suggested.

He smiled. "Very likely, Miss Cowper, since she would have consumed it at a time when he was dining away from home."

"Well," our mother said, "I'm sure it is all very dreadful and I hope that vulgar Mrs West will keep a closer eye on her daughter in future. But as for Mrs Woodstock's death, I do believe Dr King was in the right of it all along and that it was an angina that carried her off."

So that is the end of our mystery, which has provided so much material for my letters to you. It is, I admit, an unsatisfactory ending with no villain brought to justice and so many matters left unexplained. But it has given me much entertainment and has provided sufficient stuff for gossip and speculation in the town.

I fear Miss West will be quite distraught at the news of Mr Rivers' precipitate departure—I trust that the lenient hand of time (and information concerning his disgrace and subsequent lack of prospects) may bring her to see that she has had a very lucky escape. I suppose I should visit her and allow her to pour out her feelings on this matter, but fortunately the weather has altered and we have had a touch of almost everything in the way of weather; two of the severest frosts since the winter began, preceded by rain, hail and snow, so no-one, in all conscience, could expect me to venture forth in that! Perhaps, with Mr Rivers gone—Miss West (urged thereto by her mother), may yet rediscover her partiality for Mr Russell.

I feel Sir Edward is greatly put out that Mr Rivers has vanished before he could bring him to justice. But he is, I believe, a person of great persistence and will no doubt pursue him by whatever means are possible to bring this business to a more satisfactory conclusion. And it is to be hoped that Sir Matthew will be sufficiently occupied by the Duke of York to prevent his further intervention regarding his sister's death, and we may all be allowed to agree with our mother that Dr King's diagnosis was the right one—a much more comforting conclusion.

The boys are to come tomorrow to go with our father and Bates to see the water let off from the fish-pond. They are to bring each of them a spare suit of clothes so that, when the water is drained away enough, they may plunge into the mud and capture the smaller fish in landing nets and chase after the eels with eel tongs. As you know, this is a sport our father greatly enjoys and it is a sign of no small benevolence that he suggested that the boys might be allowed to accompany him. Our mother and I will, as usual, remain quietly at home.

Your visit to the exhibition at Somerset House sounds most agreeable, especially since young Mr Morton and his parents joined the party and drove you all home in their barouche. I long to hear a longer account of all your gaieties.

Yours affectionately,
E.C.

My Dear Charlotte,

The boys duly arrived for their excitements at the fish pond. Sir Edward, whom our father had also invited (as a spectator, I believe, rather than as a participant) was unable to come since Mr Woodstock's keeper had found two of the tinkers snaring rabbits in his covers and they had been taken up by the constable and were to be brought before Sir Edward, as the magistrate, that day. He waited upon us the next day, however, to thank our father, we thought, for the boys' entertainment, which, indeed, he did. But he then said he had something of a grave nature to tell us.

"One of the tinkers," he said "was caught, as you know, in Mr Woodstock's covers. Perhaps with some thought of lightening the sentence that might be given, he had a strange story to tell. He said that one day, a few weeks ago, he was (as he admitted) on his own, setting his snares when he saw Mr Russell—he described him most accurately—taking off his coat and hanging it over a bush. He then produced a pistol and shot at the sleeve of the coat, making (presumably) a tear and a powder burn. After this he took out a knife and to the tinker's amazement, made a tear in the sleeve of the shirt and then proceeded to cut his arm until the blood ran. The tinker, not wishing to betray his presence in the wood, made his escape and told no-one what he had seen."

"But why," our mother asked "should Mr Russell wish to do such a dreadful thing?"

"That I cannot tell, since I have not yet been able to speak with him. He was in Exeter performing some task for his uncle, who, as you may imagine, was still in a state of great agitation over Mr Rivers' disappearance and unable to engage in any sort of rational conversation. However, I questioned his valet, who denied all knowledge of the affair, saying merely that he had dressed the wound since his master did not want a fuss. When I asked him how his master had come to be shot, he said Mr Russell thought it must have been a poacher letting off his gun accidentally. None of this seems to me satisfactory and I have no hopes of getting to the bottom of the affair until I can come face to face with Mr Russell himself."

So you see, My Dear Charlotte, what amazing things have been happening in your absence. It is to be hoped that on your return home a more peaceful and rational state of affairs will be resumed.

I had just thought of closing this letter when Mrs Holder called in a state of great excitement. She had just come from visiting Mr Woodstock (to give him comfort she said but, more likely, to gather the latest intelligence) and had the most extraordinary news. Mr Russell has disappeared. You will not believe it—first Mr Rivers and now Mr Russell! He was expected back from Exeter before dinner-time, but he did not return and nothing has been heard of him since. Most mysteriously, Sir Edward called at Holcombe and has taken Mr Russell's valet away to be questioned. Mr Woodstock is in a state of collapse and Dr King is in permanent attendance. Needless to say, Mrs Holder only stayed with us long enough to give us her news and departed to spread the word throughout the whole of Lyme.

I will write *immediately* the next instalment of this astonishing story is available to me.

Your affectionate sister,
E.C.

My Dear Charlotte,

Faithful to my promise I take up my pen to acquaint you with the whole story. Sir Edward called upon us this morning and gave us a full account of all his findings. It seems that Corbett, Mr Russell's valet, taking fright at being questioned by Sir Edward and being privy to his master's affairs, took a horse and went to meet him on his way back from Exeter to warn him. Mr Russell told him to return to Holcombe and to pack as many of his belongings as he might conveniently transport and to meet him secretly at the White Hart in Exeter next morning. Corbett returned to Holcombe, but Sir Edward, summoned by Mr Woodstock that evening to investigate his nephew's disappearance, grew suspicious of his evasive answers and took him away to question him more closely.

The valet, now much frightened, and wishing to save his own skin, then confessed everything. The shocking fact is that it was Mr Russell who caused his aunt's death! He knew she would never pay his debts (and she was inquiring most precisely into their nature) and he felt more certain of persuading his uncle to do so. His creditors were growing more insistent so he decided he had no choice. He exchanged the laudanum bottle for an identical one containing pure opium (replacing it with the original bottle when the deed was done) and when this strong medicine caused his aunt to fall into a deep slumber he crept into her room and smothered her with a pillow.

For a while he thought he was safe, but then Sir Matthew raised doubts about his sister's death. Also he was afraid that Mr Rivers was becoming too close to Mr Woodstock and that he would supplant him. As Sir Edward's questioning became more difficult to avoid, he thought he would portray himself as the victim and staged the shooting incident, hoping, perhaps, that suspicion would fall upon Mr Rivers. He dropped hints to his uncle about the Barbados accounts (though he had no idea that they were, indeed, false) and he was, of course, delighted when Mr Rivers became alarmed and left.

Sir Edward rode straightway to the White Hart, but Mr Russell had gone. The ostler said he had hired a post-chaise and left early that morning, it seemed for London. However, even as Sir Edward was considering whether to go after him, the London mail coach arrived with news of a terrible accident—a post-chaise had lost a wheel, had run off the road and overturned, killing its driver and passenger.

You see I have given you a plain unvarnished account of these dreadful happenings, but you may well imagine our mother's exclamations and our father's anxious inquiries which punctuated the tale. For myself, I do not know what to think. I find it hard to believe anyone of our acquaintance could have acted in such a monstrous way and, indeed, he deserved to pay for what he has done. For poor Mr Woodstock's sake I believe that this ending (painful for him though it was) will relieve him of the horror of seeing his relation subjected to the necessary proceedings of the law.

Sir Edward seemed much affected by the events, holding himself responsible for Mr Russell's flight and his dreadful end, but I do not think he is in any way to blame for Mr Russell's death since he brought his end upon himself by his own wicked actions, and so I shall tell Sir Edward.

I may, however, end upon a more cheerful note. Sir Edward told us that he had heard from his cousin (as I told you, an Admiral of the White) who writes of our brother William "I have mentioned to the Board of the Admiralty his wish to be in a frigate and, from what I hear of Lord Spencer's proposals, it is certain that his promotion is likely to take place soon." Upon this good news I will end what has, otherwise, been a dismal letter. We greatly wish for your return. I hope you have enjoyed the gaieties of London and the new acquaintances you have made there and, indeed, you will miss them, but I am sure the comfort of getting back into your own room will be great.

Yours affectionately,
E.C.

11th December

My Dear Charlotte,

You may imagine the commotion the news of Mr Russell's infamy and death has caused in the neighbourhood. I felt obliged to call upon Miss West, but her mother told me that she was quite overcome and had taken to her bed (dosed no doubt with Mrs West's remedies) and could see no-one. Poor creature—to have lost not one but *two* suitors in the space of a week; it is no wonder she is quite distracted. Mrs West, too, will have to find other prey—I wonder if she will remain in Lyme to do so, or if she will return to her original hunting ground in Kent. I fear for young Mr Cooke of Axminster!

Poor Mr Woodstock was in such a state that, according to Mrs Holder, his very life seemed in danger and Dr King has been in attendance upon him every day. He now prescribes a complete change and has advised him to go at once to Bath for an indefinite period. He has recommended a lodging in Westgate Buildings, and his friend Dr Parry will arrange suitable attendance and treatment for him. Our mother has given her approval to Dr King's suggestions but Mrs Holder (not wanting Mr Woodstock away from her observations) says he would surely be happier and make a speedier recovery with his friends about him.

Later

Sir Edward arrived back from London yesterday, where he has been informing the authorities of the events of the last week. He called here this morning. As our mother was in the dairy instructing Susan on her special methods of cheese making and our father was with Bates at the farm, I was alone in the library, beginning this letter to you.

"Have you come to see my father?" I asked. "He is at the farm but I can send for him."

"Yes, I have come to see Mr Cowper—that is—I hope to see him, but, pray do not send for him yet."

He appeared agitated and began walking up and down.

"Please sir, will you not be seated?"

"Yes, yes, in a moment." He stood by the window, his back to me, then he turned suddenly and said very brusquely, "Miss Cowper I think you know very well why I am here."

"Indeed, sir?"

"Indeed, Elinor. Come now, you cannot be unaware of my feelings toward you. I am here, as I am sure you have guessed, to ask your father for permission to address you. I believe—I hope—you will not refuse to hear me. You must know what pleasure I have in your company and it is my greatest wish to enjoy that pleasure all my life. I know my circumstances are not favourable—two young boys are an undertaking that might well be considered daunting—and I am aware that the home I am offering you lacks the cheerfulness and sense of ease of that which I am asking you to leave."

He stopped suddenly and held out his hand towards me and, for some reason, I felt compelled to take it. "You must understand, sir," I said "I am only accepting your kind offer *because* of those delightful boys. You know how my mother dotes upon them and if I were to refuse the opportunity for her to become more closely related to them I am sure she would never speak to me again."

Dearest Charlotte please come home *very* soon—there are many things I wish to tell you that cannot be conveniently put in a letter. Our mother (as you may imagine) was delighted with our news and our father, giving his consent, said that he was surprised and pleased to find a sensible man who was prepared to take his frivolous daughter. Sir Edward has promised that I shall have a free hand in changing Marshwood Abbey into something more agreeable—poor man I hope he realises what he has agreed to—so I shall want your good taste to guide me in what I feel must be a complete transformation!

My heart is too full to write more, but, indeed, I am very happy.

Your affectionate sister,
E.C.

My Dear Charlotte,

Your dear letter yesterday made me very happy and I long to have you home to share in our joy. We are very glad to have the time of your and Frank's return fixed. Your trunk has arrived safely and is even now being unpacked by Lucy.

We hear that Mr Woodstock is settled in Bath and has been lately seen much in the company of a handsome widow with a grown son of six and twenty!

Your affectionate sister who signs herself for (almost) the last time,

E.C.

Lightning Source UK Ltd.
Milton Keynes UK
UKOW04f0642021215

263881UK00001B/72/P